Arnold lifted his head off the pillow. There came a gentle creaking, as of the heavy door moving, and a squeaking of a floorboard. No more.

Arnold lay back, clammy with fright. He could hear his heart hammering, as if it was in his head, not his chest.

He lay still, holding his breath to try and catch the smallest sound. His first panic had been overtaken by a rather familiar determination in the face of danger. He would have to rely on his wits now, if this was a man intending to kill him.

The ancient wooden floor sighed to the footsteps passing. A faint creak . . . there was no doubt some-one was in the room. A ray of torchlight flickered momentarily on a row of white skulls and faded. Now Arnold could hear the footsteps approaching. He held his breath. If the torch came looking under the staging, he would be lost.

He pulled the blanket right over him and held up a corner to see through. In the dim light – his eyes becoming accustomed – he saw a pair of legs walking past, very slowly . . .

Also available by K.M. Peyton:

THE WILD BOY AND QUEEN MOON
(published by Doubleday)

For older readers:

DARKLING

For younger readers:

POOR BADGER

THE BOY WHO WASN'T THERE

K.M. PEYTON

CORGI BOOKS

THE BOY WHO WASN'T THERE
A CORGI BOOK: 0 552 52717 3

First published in Great Britain by Doubleday,
a division of Transworld Publishers Ltd

PRINTING HISTORY
Doubleday edition published 1992
Corgi edition published 1993

Set in 11pt Century Schoolbook by
Chippendale Type Ltd, Otley, West Yorkshire

Corgi Books are published by Transworld Publishers Ltd,
61-63 Uxbridge Road, London W5 5SA,
in Australia by Transworld Publishers (Australia) Pty Ltd,
15-25 Helles Avenue, Moorebank, NSW 2170,
and in New Zealand by Transworld Publishers (NZ) Ltd,
3 William Pickering Drive, Albany, Auckland.

Printed and bound in Great Britain by
Cox & Wyman Ltd, Reading, Berks.

To Graham

CHAPTER ONE

When Arnold Bracegirdle ran away from the delinquents' home for the fourth time he made for his Great Aunt Margaret's in the forlorn hope that no-one would find him there. Unsurprised, she said she would hand him in, but later, because she was too busy at the moment to wait in for 'those people'. First he could help her with the garden party at Bosky Hollow, where she was doing the catering. He could carry the food in from the van and help her lay it out on the trestle tables on the lawn.

Bosky Hollow's lawns ran down to a lake. This was a mile or two away from where Aunt Margaret lived, in East Anglia, the most boring place in the world, Arnold thought, but useful if 'they' were looking for you in Barking, where he lived with his mum when she was there, and his grandma when she wasn't. Bosky Hollow was a sumptuous bungalow in a lane with a lot of trees and exotic shrubs; the houses were almost hidden, with drives winding up to olde oake front doors with huge glass porches full of potted plants. Arnold slaved diligently for a couple of hours to-ing and fro-ing for Aunt Margaret, the only person in the world he quite liked, and then, as the guests started to arrive, she told him to keep out of the way, so he went down to look at the lake.

He actually felt rather woozy, having sampled Aunt Margaret's punch – liking it, he had drunk more than a sample. It was now living up to its name. He sat down on the water's edge, nicely sheltered by some banks of rhododendrons, and started to consider his present situation. Not bad really. Arnold only thought of the immediate present, never of the past nor the future, and he liked the lake and its warm evening smell, and the party lights twinkling in the trees round the house, and the hum of conversation as the guests started to crowd the manicured lawns behind him. He had a pocketful of sausage rolls and assorted 'bites' to keep starvation at bay and enough punch inside him to rose-tint the situation.

It was at this happy moment in his life that he saw the dead body float into view.

He thought at first it was a deck-chair, but deck-chairs didn't wear evening dress. He then assumed he was drunk. He shut his eyes and sobered his thoughts, and looked again. It was a very dead body, drifting past. The lake seemed to have a current on it and the body gave a sort of roll as it came near and Arnold saw a blueish face with open, dark eyes and a handsome hookish nose with green weed trailing, caught, and fanned-out black hair like trailing fishnet. There was a white hand with fat white fingers and a diamond ring, a white cuff, all very ethereal. Very dead. Arnold stopped eating his sausage roll and felt rather queer. He stood up. The people far away up the lawn, behind the shrubs, seemed to go round in circles. He wished someone was nearer.

Behind the shrubs, two gardens along, a girl about his own age was playing the violin. She had a music stand facing the lake, and was playing, very earnestly, tuneless sort of stuff with a lot of twiddles. The body was going her way. Arnold shoved his way through the shrubs to try and alert her.

'I say – er—'

'What are you doing in my garden?'

'There's a body—'

'A what?' She was thin and wiry and blonde and had very fierce blue eyes.

'There. Look!' He pointed.

The current had taken it out quite a bit

9

and it was hard to make out in the dusk.

'It's a deck-chair,' she said.

'No. Honestly. It's a dead body. I saw it quite close.'

'Who are you?'

'It doesn't matter, does it?' What a berk she was! 'Can't you see it's a body?'

To give her her due, she tried, staring out over the water. But even Arnold could see it was hopeless to make out now, like a waterlogged mattress, drifting. It was too dark.

'I'm at that party,' he said. 'I saw it. That's all.' He felt stupid now.

'Well, if you think I'm going to get involved— I haven't got time. I've got to get my practice in.'

'You can do that later.'

'It's already later. We're going on tour tomorrow. I'm in an orchestra,' she added.

He thought she looked too young.

'A schools orchestra,' she added. 'We're going to Scotland.'

He stood dithering and she then said, rather nastily, 'Now run off and tell the police, but leave me out of it. They'll be awfully pleased.'

Ring the police was exactly what he could not do. They'd ask for his name. He pushed his way back through the bushes, smarting slightly from his acerbic encounter. Who did she think she was, so sarky and stuck-up? Not interested in dead bodies . . . such cool was rather impressive. He made for his Aunt Margaret, who was handing a plateful of things on sticks to a small group of foreign-looking gentlemen.

'There's a dead body in the lake. I saw it. A man with black hair and a diamond ring.'

Afterwards he supposed if he hadn't been drinking the punch and his intelligence hadn't been impaired he would have kept mum. His announcement was not taken with much joy. His aunt gave him a look that made his blood run cold and the foreign gentlemen stared at him as if he was something nasty they had trodden in.

'Excuse me.' Aunt Margaret smiled at the group, turned and propelled Arnold sharply out of earshot with scratchy fingers round the back of his neck.

'Are you mad?' she hissed.

'No. There is. I saw it.'

'This is neither the time nor the place to find dead bodies. You are here on sufferance and I am only the caterer. You've been drinking the punch, haven't you?'

She gave him a shake.

'Yes, but—'

'Even if it's true, which I very much doubt, it will be found without your assistance – this lake is surrounded by houses. Now just stop making an exhibition of yourself. Take this plate round and when you've done that you'd better go home. There's a path back to the village across the fields – you'll see a stile and a sign just down the lane, turn left out of the front gate. I'll be here till late and you ought to be in bed.'

She gave him a doorkey.

'It's my spare. Now don't lose it.'

She shoved the plate of titbits at him and gave him a push. He wandered off into the crowd and found himself back with the foreign gentlemen. He proffered his plate. They smiled genially.

'You go to the police station about this body you see?'

'Yes,' he lied. 'I'm going on the way home.'

He didn't want to seem a complete prat. One had to have the courage of one's convictions when it came to dead bodies. Of course there was no way he could go to the police, but he would have if he could.

They smiled at him indulgently. He scowled back and passed on to another group. The bits went quite quickly; he ate the last ten or so and put the plate back with the empties. He was now a free agent.

The party was getting loud and crowded and it was now pitch dark. He decided to have one last look at the lake before he departed, in case with any luck the body was there for all to see at the bottom of the garden. He went down between the bushes and stood peering along the shore. Nothing to be seen.

But somewhere along a bit, the opposite way from the violin girl (who seemed to have given up) he heard the noise of a boat being pushed into the water and oars being fixed in rowlocks. There was a subdued murmuring of male voices, urgent, and then the faint splash of oars. Arnold backed away and crouched in the rhododendrons. It was too dark to see much but he thought he could make out a rowing boat with two men in it. The men seemed to gleam white at the throat, as if they too wore evening dress, but by now Arnold no longer trusted his senses. He decided it was time to go home and sleep it off.

He skirted the party and went out into the lane to look for the stile and the track across the field. He had been this way before in times past – happier times when he was still a good boy and his mother loved him and hadn't run off with Carl the bus-driver – so, although it was very dark, he knew the general direction. The beaten line of the path could be made out across the grass, leading towards the dark blotch of the woods beyond and the few lights of the village.

Arnold, at home with night-time business, nevertheless found country dark a good deal more uneasy than town dark. He was an urban creature born and bred, streetwise, up to all the tricks. The present wide spaces, the powerful silence, the earthy, dewdripping coldness in his nostrils, made him nervous. This was not his scene. There seemed to be some animals in the field – cows? – whose white shapes glimmered ghostlike in the distance against the deeper darkness of hedge and lowering tree . . . how uncivilized it was! Arnold recalled, with a wrench of nostalgia, the smell of traffic and hot tarmac, hotdogs and festering dustbins. He was dead scared of cows.

He hurried, head down, and had an unaccountable feeling that someone was following him. He glanced behind several times. There seemed to be a white shape like evening dress again . . . impossible . . . too slender for a cow. Certainly there were cows, or worse. He could hear the tearing of grass and sensed the gleam of animal eyes. He broke into a jog, feeling the sweat rising. The animals drew closer. He thought he attracted them, running; they were curious. He could smell their breath, he thought, their warm, fetid cow smell. He glanced behind again, and the figure that wasn't a cow was still there, closer. Panic flared. He ran for the line of trees and now heard footsteps – undeniably footsteps – coming up behind. He was so scared he shouted out.

He could run when anyone was after him but this time the figure was larger than life and evil, and caught him from behind by the throat. Arnold came up short, throttled, his head wrenched backwards. He felt he was caught by claws. Putting up his hands to pull the claws away, he encountered fur. The claws dug into his Adam's apple. He tried to scream and could only gargle, so frightened he could almost feel himself passing out with pure funk. Whatever it was that held him, it had deadly intentions. It smelled of whisky, yet had the hands of a gorilla.

Arnold could feel his breath denied, his eyes bulging in his head. His ears roared. It was like going under deep water, fighting upwards, choking, drowning. Yet above him were stars in a serene sky. He flung himself backwards against his attacker, the only movement open to him, held as he was by the throat and unable to turn. All his remaining strength went into a wild heave and the next moment his throat was free and he was turning a backward somersault over something large and warm and hairy that seemed to come out of the very ground itself.

Arnold filled his lungs with air and screamed. He now had his face hard in wet grass, soil on his lips, rolling over and over. Something very painful trod on the small of his back, pinning him momentarily, and the dark shadow of his adversary let forth an inhuman bellow. Arnold froze into a ball. Above him the disturbed animal charged, clipping him a parting kick; the gorilla ran and Arnold, seeing his chance, got to his feet and belted for the dark sanctuary of the woods. There was a stile which he vaulted over, a path of leafmould and mud which muffled his flying footsteps. He was choking and crying and gulping with fright, terrified the gorilla was coming after him, but after a bit he lost the path in a sea of brambles and came to a halt. He was shaking so much he thought his knees would give way.

All was silence around him. He held his breath and listened, and heard only the soft soughing of a breeze in the branches above him and, far far away, borne by the same breeze, the murmur and laughter from the party he had left. He could not believe what had happened. Was he dreaming it? He put his hand up to his burning throat, and felt sticky blood on his fingers. It appeared to be oozing from long scratches down his neck and his throat felt as if the hangman had been practising on it. This was no figment of his imagination. But what had attacked him? He had no idea and the memory of it set his teeth chattering again.

He ran the rest of the way through the wood and came out thankfully on to the street which ran into the village. His aunt's modest cottage was one of the first he came to. He let himself in, locked the door behind him and switched all the lights on.

His adventure had knocked all the stuffing out of him. He looked at his face in the mirror and frightened himself: drawn white cheeks, staring dark eyes, deep puncture marks on his throat still oozing blood, and the beginnings of raw bruises below his ears. He mopped the blood away with his aunt's dishcloth. He then felt so shaky he went to bed.

He must have slept for, a long time later, his aunt put her head round the door. Arnold woke and pulled the sheet tight up round his ears, quick reactions having been learned the hard way.

'I forgot to tell you, dear, but there were bullocks in that field. I hope they didn't frighten you?'

He did not reply. First time he knew bullocks had claws.

'Goodnight, dear. We'll talk about everything tomorrow.'

CHAPTER TWO

Arnold found a red woollen scarf of his aunt's and wrapped it round his neck before he went down to breakfast.

'What on earth are you wearing that for?' she asked.

'I've got a sore throat.'

'Let's see. Open your mouth.'

He obliged and she peered into his healthy tonsils.

'Hmm.'

She gave him her usual wary, nervous look. Unmarried Aunt Margaret couldn't fathom Arnold, but had a nice, tolerant nature and wished – in vain – that she could do something to help him. She thought he would thrive in the country, away from Bad Influences, but Arnold rudely said he would die of boredom within the week. He only came to her as a last resort, for sanctuary. He was an under-nourished, white-faced, townie rat to her way of thinking, small for his thirteen years, perky, stubborn and dangerous. He had bright inquisitive eyes and dark hair that stood up like a lavatory brush. Margaret's niece Maudie had had him by mistake during one of her sporadic marriages – a feckless girl and a useless mother in her aunt's opinion. How could one expect the lad to be a good boy with the example he was set?

'What are we going to do with you?' she sighed.

Usually Arnold just stayed until he got so bored he went off home and got into trouble again.

'I'll just lie low for a bit,' he said.

'I've got to go to the cash and carry this morning. You'll just have to amuse yourself.'

'Can I come?'

'Certainly not.'

She had taken him once and been shocked to find what he had managed to steal and hide in his pockets during the outing.

'You can keep the key then, in case I'm held up. Go for a nice walk. Some fresh air would do you good by the look of you.' She peered at him closely and shook her head. 'You look terrible.'

Arnold decided against showing her his vampire-ridden neck. In daylight the claw-marks scared him rigid. The attack in the field had definitely been no figment of his imagination.

'You didn't really see a body in the lake last night? I could have murdered you, blurting it out—'

But it hadn't been Aunt Margaret who had tried to murder him.

He shrugged.

'It was very naughty of you, in front of those guests. Now just you behave yourself while I'm out.'

This was a very boring prospect. After watching television for a couple of hours Arnold decided to go back to the lake and see if he could see the body again. It had a morbid fascination for him; after all, one did not see a dead body every day of the week. He also thought it would be quite fun to get down to the lake via the gardens of the smart houses, dodging through the shrubberies like a private detective, and creeping along the shore without being seen. It was the country equivalent of crawling over warehouse roofs and dropping through skylights.

So he went out into the cold country air, amazed afresh by the utter dreariness of all that grass and silence. There was nobody about save a muffled figure on a motorbike looking at some malfunction of the works on the side of the road, and a woman about two hundred years old pulling a trolley towards the village shop. Arnold decided to forego the short cut with the bulls –

and worse – and take the long way round the lane. He rather thought it was a bull that had saved his life the night before, by frightening off the gorilla, but the incident was all a bit hazy now and, if it hadn't been for the marks round his neck, he would have put it down to being intoxicated and scared of the dark.

He wandered along the lane. The motorbike came past him just as a car came along. The motorbike looked as if it would mow him down, but had to slow up sharply for the car. Arnold thought a motorbike would be a bit of all right and wondered, if he stole one, would he be able to start it and ride it away? Doubtful, without a bit of practice first. It would be worth getting to know how to ride one, for when he got the chance of 'finding' one. Did Aunt Margaret know a boy with a motorbike? He'd ask when he got back.

He came out on to the road where the smart houses were, those running down to the lake. It was very quiet, like a graveyard Arnold thought. The motorbike was coming back. Who was this geezer? Arnold got on to the pavement and to his amazement the motorbike did a wheelie up the kerb and came straight at him, accelerating with a great crackle of engine-power.

If Arnold – he thought afterwards – had been a slow-witted country lad he would have been a goner. As it was, with a lifetime of practice in jumping on and off buses between lights, swinging on the backs of lorries, running from the clutches of irate shopkeepers and other gymnastics required by his way of life, instinct bade him jump into the flowering currants of 'Meadowview' within an ace of being run down. The smell of scorching rubber and hot engine filled his quivering nostrils as he rolled under the freshly manured bushes.

'Someone's trying to kill me!' was the not unnatural conclusion that filled his reeling brain. He dared not move, listening to the sound of the fading motorbike engine. If it turned and came back he'd have to make a run for it and ring a smart doorbell.

'I say, are you all right?'

A pair of be-jeaned legs came into his vision beyond the bushes. A bent head, peering, met his frightened gaze. It looked like the violin girl.

'That bike tried to run you down. Is he some mate of yours, playing tricks? Looked jolly dangerous to me.'

Arnold rolled out and scrambled to his feet. He smelled of manure. The girl wrinkled her nose.

'Oh, it's you.'

'Someone's trying to kill me!' Arnold squeaked.

'A joke, surely?'

Remembering the dead body, she was obviously putting him down as a hysteric. He pulled the red scarf aside to reveal his vampire marks.

'Someone tried to strangle me on the way home last night!'

The girl went rather white. 'Ugh!' Then, 'I *say*!' with considerable sympathy. 'You look awful,' she added. 'You can come home, if you like – there's no-one in. Only me.'

Arnold accepted the invitation gratefully, feeling that two attempts on his life within twelve hours justified the acceptance of some soft living. Her house was even plusher than Bosky Hollow, big enough to bed the whole population of his street at home by the look of it. She took him into the kitchen, a vast warm purring laboratory sort of place, and pulled out a chair for him at a large pine table.

'Here, I'll make you a coffee. Who are you? You're not from around here?'

He gave her a sanitized version of his appearance at Aunt Margaret's and told her about the gorilla attack of the night before. She studied his neck with deep interest.

'That's serious!'

'Yeah.'

'So was just now. Really serious. You must tell the police.'

'I'd rather not. They wouldn't believe me. They don't like me. I don't like them.' In a nutshell. The girl didn't argue.

'I'd rather just disappear,' Arnold said. 'It's not healthy round here.'

'It might be something to do with that body last night. You said you saw a body?'

'That's right! I did. And I told a few geezers at the party and they said, was I going to tell the police, and I said yes, when I got home.'

'There you are!'

'I think I'll disappear for a while.'

'Come with us! The coach is leaving at lunchtime. Next stop the Highlands of Scotland – no-one'll find you there!'

'How can I?'

'Easy! Sixty of us in two coaches – all from different schools, different countries even – nobody will notice one more! You can take my old violin in its case and pretend you're part of the orchestra!'

Arnold gaped. The girl's cornflower eyes shone. How was he to know she liked diversion and excitement in her life? Her boredom threshold was abnormally low; her father was a top seed tennis player, at present in America, who had made millions and let her spend whatever she liked; her mother was temporarily in the south of France and the 'minder' who was supposed to be looking after her had gone to London for the day to buy a wedding outfit.

'Nothing to it! Even the people looking after us

don't know who we are, do they? We're all from different schools. We're going to stay somewhere for a few days, rehearsing all day, then we're going to play a few concerts around Scotland and then come home. It couldn't be a better way to disappear!'

'I can't play the violin,' Arnold said feebly.

'Don't be so stupid! Just carry it about. You needn't come to rehearsals, no-one'll notice in that mob.'

Her eyes were now positively sparkling with excitement. She was jumping about the kitchen like a grasshopper.

'It's a great idea! It's not as if we'll be alone. I've got friends – we'll meet them on the bus – ones I like in the orchestra, ones I've got to know. They'll help – they'll love it. There's a really tough girl who plays the cymbals, and a clarinettist who's brilliant – clever, I mean. He can cope with anything. They'll see you OK. We'll all see you OK. It'll be terrific fun!'

Arnold wasn't at all sure about the fun, but a coach ride to the Highlands of Scotland starting at lunchtime seemed a very attractive idea. After that he could do a runner. Go to Glasgow. He had a cousin in Glasgow. Glasgow was a homely sort of place.

'What's your name?' the girl asked suddenly.

'Arnold.'

'Ugh.'

'What's yours?'

'Jodie.'

'Ugh.'

They considered each other, taking in the idea of what they had just planned. Arnold felt a bit funny in the pit of his stomach, wondering what he was in for. And who wanted to kill him? The vision of the motorbike rearing at him across the pavement was going to stay with him for a long time. He felt quite trembly and rather sick.

Jodie said, quite kindly, 'Whoever it is, you'll be all right once we're away. I'll find you some things to take.' She glanced at her watch. 'The taxi'll be here in half an hour.'

Uncertain as he was, Arnold was swayed by Jodie's authoritative manner. She took him upstairs with her to her bedroom and packed him a holdall of T-shirts, jerseys and pairs of jeans. She had racks and drawersful of bright-coloured clothes and her jeans fitted Arnold perfectly.

'An anorak . . . take your pick.' She opened another wardrobe.

Arnold chose one in a camouflaging grey-green, hoping he wouldn't show up against the Highlands, which he assumed were greenish.

Jodie pulled a violin case out of a locker under her bed.

'Here, you can carry that. No-one'll ask any questions, I bet. The woman in charge – Mrs Knox she's called – doesn't know any of us by sight. Even our conductor, he can never remember who's who. People come and go rather in this sort of orchestra.'

Jodie went into her father's room and came back with an armful of underpants and pairs of pyjamas. They were all rather swamping but Jodie insisted on stuffing them in.

'I don't want all that!' Arnold tended to wear the same clothes for a week at a time.

'You don't have to carry it – it'll all go in the coach.'

She was like a steamroller, Arnold decided. When he had recovered from his near misses at being murdered he would have to stand up to her. Girls should be kept in their place. But for the time being it suited him to be swept away to Scotland.

The taxi arrived and Jodie locked up the house. In spite of himself Arnold was impressed by her utter familiarity with organizing her own life. She was as independent as he was. She appeared to be as neglected by her elders and betters as himself, in spite of coming from an obviously rich family. Very odd. He thought only dropouts from dumbo families like his own got that sort of treatment. He sat in the back of the taxi wondering whether perhaps he was in some sort of a dream. Nothing felt real at all.

The taxi decanted them into the car park of a large school some ten miles away, where two coaches were parked, surrounded by a milling crowd of young people and their parents. Total chaos reigned.

'What did I tell you?' Jodie said. 'Think anyone'll notice one more in this mob? Come on, let's get some decent seats. And I'll see if I can collar my mates.'

She shoved Arnold ahead of her, so that they stowed their luggage in the bowels of the coach and fought their way aboard. The stalwart Mrs Knox stood at the door of the coach ticking off names.

'Jodie Angmering. David Smith,' said Jodie firmly.

Mrs Knox ticked them off and allowed them to pass.

'Who's David Smith?' Arnold muttered.

'Oh, he's a stupid lad, plays the trombone. If she asks any questions we'll say he's on the other coach. If she counts us, you can duck down.'

She seemed to have no nerves at all. Arnold let himself be swept to the back of the coach, shoved bodily into the corner seat. Jodie seemed to collar required reinforcements on her way down the coach: a stout girl with black corkscrew curls in a great springing mass round her head, a weedy little boy with pimples and a worried expression, and an elegant youth somewhat older than the rest of them, blond and cool.

'This is Christian Persimmon,' Jodie introduced him to Arnold. 'Clarinet. Nutty McTavish, cymbals.' This was the girl with the corkscrew curls. The wimpy lad was, 'Hoomey Rossitor. Triangle and wood-block. The limit of his talent.'

'You watch it, Jodie Angmering,' said Nutty belligerently. 'Someone's got to play 'em.'

'The theory is that brass, cymbals, triangles and likewise uncouth noises are given to dolts to balance the brilliance of the strings and wind. School orchestras have to be seen to be fair to all levels of intelligence.'

Nutty hit Jodie with a canvas bag she was carrying so that Jodie lost her balance and fell under the seat. Mrs Knox could be heard counting: 'Sixteen, seventeen, eighteen . . . '

Jodie got up again as the voice faded into the general uproar.

'This is Arnold,' she said. 'Someone is trying to murder him. You won't believe this. Show them, Arnold.'

Arnold pulled his scarf down to reveal his strangle marks. They all stared, obviously impressed.

'And this morning, a motorbike – I saw it –

tried to run him down. Really meant it. So I said come with me, out of range.'

Jodie's authority impressed her friends: they took her news seriously. But Christian then put the obvious questions: 'Who is Arnold? Where's he sprung from? Why doesn't he tell his parents? Why doesn't he go to the police?' He turned his superior face to Arnold and examined him in a schoolmasterly way. His eyes were a pale grey-green, very intelligent.

'Can't go to the police,' Arnold mumbled.

'Ho,' said Nutty. 'We know people like that, don't we, Hoomey?'

'Like Nails, you mean? He's OK now.'

'Arnold found a body last night,' Jodie explained. 'He told various persons he'd found a body and they laughed at him, so he said he was going to tell the police. I think that's why one of them tried to stop him.'

'Cor!' Hoomey was greatly impressed. Nutty was looking slightly sceptical.

'Where did you see a body?'

Arnold explained about the party. He told them he thought he saw a rowing boat launched before he departed for home.

'Was it really a body?'

'Yes, for sure it was. A bloke in evening dress.'

By this time the coach had set off and was putting out into green countryside. Arnold, squashed into the corner of the back seat, felt greatly relieved to be departing from the scene of his latest adventures. Whatever might happen to him in this orchestra muddle, it would be of small consequence compared to being murdered.

The coach was completely full. A fair sprinkling of adults were amongst the young, all yakking hard and making almost as much noise as the orchestral players. A stocky red-headed boy of about Arnold's age was making his way to the back of the coach, peering at all the occupants. He stopped by Jodie and said, 'You seen David Smith? Mrs Knox says he got on this coach.'

'No, he's on the other one,' Jodie said.

'She doesn't know if she's coming or going,' the boy said.

He squashed up Christian and Nutty and sat down. He looked at Arnold curiously.

'Who he?'

'Arnold. Arnold, this is John Pike. Timpanist.'

'Drums,' said Nutty kindly, as Arnold failed to comprehend.

'What do you play?'

'He doesn't play. He's on the run from a murderer.'

Jodie went into her explanations again and Arnold wondered if, by the time they got to Scotland, the whole coach would know who he was and why.

'You going to tell everyone?' he muttered.

'No,' said Jodie. 'Only us. John is one of Us. That's it, the five of us. We stick together.'

John Pike looked on a fairly high plane of intelligence, like Christian. They went to the same school apparently, an expensive boarding school in the Midlands. It obviously taught them this cool style. Nutty and Hoomey went to some dim school they called the Gasworks where they were encouraged in 'out of school activities'. The two of them obviously thought that a murder hunt, coming under this umbrella, was far more interesting than playing cymbals or triangle. Nutty's pebbly eyes gleamed with excitement. She was obviously a doer, a goer, with her strong body, tossing mane of extraordinary hair, and enthusiasm. Jodie, used to being the boss, treated her with a certain amount of respect and caution.

'I bet we could hide him in the orchestra, no trouble,' Nutty said. 'Up at the back with us timps. Pikey's only got to throw his drum cover over him – no-one'd see him.'

'Or give him a violin in the back row,' Christian said scornfully. 'No-one hears their squeaking, luckily. He'd only have to wave his bow about like the rest of 'em.' He grinned at Jodie.

She glared back. 'You be careful!' Then added, 'I've given him a violin actually, just in case.'

'In case what?' Arnold said.

'Well, in case we can't manage it without you coming to rehearsals with us. You never know. You'd be better hidden in the orchestra than staying behind somewhere on your own.'

Arnold shrank down in his seat, horror flooding him. A member of an orchestra was not his scene, no way.

'You want to stay alive, don't you?' Jodie's sky-blue eyes needled him.

'But I'll be OK once I'm away! That murdering lot – the idea is we've left 'em behind, surely?'

John Pike said, slowly, 'Do you know something?'

'What?'

'That party last night . . . was it the one at that Bosky Hollow place?'

'Yeah, that's it.'

'You reckon that's where the murderer was, who came after you?'

'Yes, of course. It all fits,' Jodie said impatiently.

'I'll tell you something,' said John Pike, grinning. 'That party was a fund-raising do for this orchestra. My dad was invited. Didn't you know that? Half the people at that party are now on this trip. Your murderer's probably sitting up front there.'

Arnold went white.

Nutty's eyes gleamed even more brilliantly. 'I say, we can track him down! Give us something to think about – *really* think about! He'll have no idea we're on to him!'

The boys all looked highly interested but Jodie, like Arnold, was stunned. She looked wanly across at him.

'Perhaps it wasn't such a good idea after all . . . '

CHAPTER THREE

The two coaches sped on through the night. It was high summer but the rain beat on the windows and clouds of spray plumed across the motorways, obliterating all signs and direction boards. Arnold had planned to do a runner at Glasgow but, his geography being dismal, he had no way of knowing which was Glasgow out of the urban conglomerations they passed. Whenever they left the coach for snacks and toilets, they seemed to be in desolate countryside. No doubt he was uneasily asleep if and when they passed Glasgow, for when he awoke at dawn the Highlands seemed to have arrived: wavering horizons through the teeming rain of endless grass and forest – not, to Arnold's eyes a pretty sight.

The thought of branching out on his own in this alien land was not attractive. He had friends and protectors, food, warmth and comfort where he was, which counted for a good deal. In fact it was a long time since so many people had become so interested in him.

On the last boring leg of the journey Arnold told them the story of his life and admitted that he was on the run from various authorities, no doubt being actively looked for, so they occupied themselves by choosing a new name for him. Arnold had rather thought he was going to disappear and wouldn't need a name but Nutty insisted.

'We've got time now. It might come in useful, you never know. And anyway, with a name like that, you ought to be pleased to change it. Arnold Bracegirdle is a hopeless name. You might as well be called Corsets as Bracegirdle.'

'Arnold is Ronald another way,' Hoomey said.

'Dralon,' said John Pike.

'That's stuff you make curtains out of.'

'Dralon Corsets.'

'Crosset. Dralon Crosset,' said John Pike.

'Bracegirdle could trace back to armour. Not corsets at all,' said Christian. Arnold thought this a more intelligent contribution.

'Ironside,' said John Pike.

'Dralon Ironside.'

'Not Dralon!'

'Ironside's all right.'

'It's a bit noticeable,' Nutty said. 'He doesn't really want to stand out.'

'Ron Crosset. That's harmless enough,' Jodie said. 'D'you like that?' she demanded.

'Ron Crosset's all right.'

'We'll call you Ron then. Say you come from the same school as Nutty and Hoomey if anyone asks. They've got no hangers-on on board, have they?'

'No.'

Arnold tried to think himself into being Ron. Mostly his friends called him Arn. It wasn't very different. His enemies probably didn't know his name anyway, but changing it wasn't a bad idea. Who were his enemies?

'They were foreign,' he remembered.

'Lots of foreigners on board,' Jodie said. 'We've got three French boys, with two teachers, two Germans, the Russian boy wonder and his minders – three of them – two Scandinavians in charge of the instruments . . . lots.'

No gorillas. How come he was strangled with claws?

'Gorillas don't have claws,' John Pike pointed out, when the subject was discussed. 'Bears have claws.'

But the claw marks were very impressive evidence. Arnold thought, without them no-one would have taken him seriously.

The coaches were now making their way down a minor winding road towards the Dee valley where it seemed they were going to stay in an old hunting lodge. They trundled over a long bridge and through some ancient wrought iron gates, and a large complex of buildings lay ahead: a huge grim stone house with four storeys, small mean windows and high, ancient chimneys tossing off plumes of horizontal smoke; barns and old stable buildings making a large courtyard before it, along with a row of workers' cottages that stretched down to the bridge. In front of the complex was the wide, rapidly flowing river and a grass valley dotted with grazing deer, and behind and all round, the hills rose up to close with the low, scudding grey clouds. The rain tipped down. When the coaches came to a halt and the engines were turned off, Arnold was not the only face which took in the scene with less than enthusiasm. The driver opened the doors and cold air smelling of wet grass and woodsmoke blew bracingly into the fug.

Mrs Knox stood up and smiled encouragingly.

'Now, we're all rather tired and hungry! We're going straight in to have breakfast and after that we'll see about settling ourselves in!'

To Arnold, never having left London in his life save to go to Aunt Margaret's, the place was like something out of an old telly film, completely unreal. He expected to see men in kilts with meat cleavers in their hands waiting in the hall . . .

but no, only soft-voiced ladies and hearty school-teachers directing them to long trestle tables set for breakfast. The floor was of bare stone flags and a vast fireplace stood at the top end burning whole trees by the look of it, yet not making any great impression on the atmosphere of stale damp that prevailed. Large tin teapots with steaming spouts arriving at each end of the tables looked more encouraging. Arnold's new friends carried him along in the shoving crowd to get a place together in the queue for food and they were given huge plates of bacon and eggs and fried bread and tomatoes. Spirits rose rapidly. At the bottom of one of the tables another place was being laid and a lady was saying, 'So sorry, we must have counted wrong.'

Stuffed with good food, a steaming mug of tea in his hand, Arnold realized that he was on to a good thing, and became increasingly worried as to whether he was going to be quick-witted enough to remain undiscovered. The dead body and the murder attempt took second place to taking in the difficulties that lay ahead.

'I think you all know the timetable for the first week,' a geezer was saying to the assembly. 'Rehearsing in the morning; outings, sport or free time in the afternoon; recitals and lectures in the evening. There is a large plan of the complex at the bottom of the hall to show you where everything takes place. The main music hall, where we shall have rehearsals of the whole orchestra, is in the old ballroom which is a separate building on the edge of the deer park – a very historical building, by the way, you will learn more about it later. There are various rooms allocated for separate practising on the first floor; the second floor is the adults' accommodation – no intrusion here please, without appointment. We want to get some peace – it's our holiday too, remember. Your dormitories are on the third floor, females to the right of the central staircase, males to the left. The day's timetable will be posted by the front door here. This morning you can settle in, find your way around, and be back here for lunch at one o'clock.'

Naturally there was a rude stampede to the dormitories, to bag the best rooms and beds next to best friends. Arnold found that Christian was a man of great authority. Without even seeming to hurry, he was there first, not having lost his way like three-quarters of the others, and in charge of the best bedroom without turning a hair. No-one disputed his right. He stood at the door repulsing hopeful invaders with his cool, scornful stare.

There were four beds in the room, a mix of camp-beds and sagging divans with motley covers. Christian and his friend John Pike accepted the company of Hoomey and Arnold with a certain resignation, seeing that Hoomey was lost without his minder Nutty, and Arnold was lost full stop. Arnold could see that Hoomey was destined to be his mate, not a happy thought, for Hoomey was a wimp of the first order. It was a wonder he didn't have his teddy bear with him. John Pike had the same authoritative air as Christian: natural leaders of men, but quite nice with it. Christian was older, sixteen or seventeen by the look of him, with an almost pretty face with its sensitive features and clear, long-lashed eyes. Straight blond hair fell untidily over his forehead. His sport was, apparently, polo. Blimey, Arnold thought, I've got myself up a funny cul-de-sac here. He sat on his lumpy bed wondering whether he wasn't dreaming it all.

'This is your bed. Tailormade,' John Pike said to Arnold, opening the door of a huge wardrobe. 'Snuggle down in the bottom here and no-one'll ever find you.'

'And shut the door, you mean?' Terror rose in Arnold at the thought.

John Pike examined the latch. 'With a bit of wire you could open it from inside. It just might be useful, you never know. Leave it open at night, but if anyone comes in we can close it and they'll never know.'

Jodie and Nutty, visiting, thought it a great idea.

'How come you got such a smart room then?' Nutty asked crossly.

The window in the massively thick wall was in the gable of the great house and had a commanding view down the valley to the west, away from such civilization as there was. The wide river snaked down from its mysterious source in the high mountains beyond, which seemed layered one behind the other in receding shades of rain-dimmed purple. By contrast with the cold magnificence outside, the room was quite cosy, with an ancient red carpet on the floor, an even more ancient radiator exuding a faint warmth, two nineteen-twenties armchairs in faded gold plush covers and a table.

'Four beds, all the same. You'll get someone else shoved in. That'll mean explaining Arnold. Ron, I mean.'

'Oh, we'll sort that out,' said Christian airily.

'We've got to find out who's trying to murder him,' Jodie said.

'Must we?' said John Pike.

'Let's wait till they try again,' Christian said with a grin.

'It'll be fun hiding him, a bit of a challenge,' Nutty said. 'Make life more interesting.'

Arnold found their attitude less than encouraging, but all the same liked the feeling of being one of a gang. He was quite content to be carried along, not quite knowing what was going to happen. It was quite a familiar feeling, not knowing what to expect. He felt far less frightened of whatever it was that threatened him, no longer alone. Even if it was, on the surface of it, safer to go back home again, he did not want to leave his new friends. They seemed to make all the decisions too, which was restful. Apart from Hoomey, they were very pushy types, very sure of themselves.

They all went to collect their luggage. Arnold staggered up the stairs with his holdall and the violin. Christian brought his clarinet but John Pike had to see to the removal of his drums to the ballroom-cum-rehearsal-room where they were to live. Nobody so far seemed to be claiming the fourth bed.

'Holy cow, you should see that ballroom!' John Pike said when he came back. 'It's really creepy. It's got two thousand skulls in it, all mounted round the walls and on the ceiling.'

'Skulls?'

'Deer, you know. Antlers on bits of head with empty eye-sockets, peering at you everywhere you look.'

They took this in. It seemed excessively foreign.

Arnold plonked his gear on the fourth bed, but Jodie told him to leave it clear for a bit.

'You're bound to get a fourth person. They're still scrimmaging up the corridor.'

No sooner had she spoken the words than Mrs Knox put her head round the door with one of her eternal lists.

'Any spare beds in here?'

'One,' said Jodie.

'Ah.' She consulted the list and stared at them all closely. 'You're visiting?' she said to the girls. 'And one of you is visiting?' to the boys.

'He is,' said Jodie, nodding at Arnold.

'Who is he?' Mrs Knox consulted her list.

'David Smith.'

'Ah.'

Arnold could feel his heart racing uncomfortably. Mrs Knox had certainly got his measure with her intent peer. Had she already ticked off David Smith? Jodie knew she had taken a risk and cursed herself for not keeping Arnold hidden until all the settling-in had finished. But Mrs Knox turned her gaze not to Arnold but to Christian and John Pike.

'So, you look like a responsible couple. I'm looking for a bed for the Russian boy. His people want him to stay with them, but what's the point of his doing a tour like this if he lives apart?

He needs to get to know you young people and learn the language. He'll never do that unless he mixes. But he seems very nervous and wound-up. I'm a bit worried about him, to tell the truth. Are you prepared to take a little trouble to help him settle in?'

The two boys exchanged glances.

Mrs Knox said, 'He speaks not a word of English. I suppose you don't know any Russian?'

'No.'

'It's not fashionable any more, is it? Well, you'll just have to do your best. I'll go and fetch him.'

She left the room and they all looked at each other glumly.

'That's all we need!' said Jodie. 'Hiding Arnold and trying to explain what he's doing in the bottom of the wardrobe to someone who doesn't speak English!'

Christian grinned. 'Might be a bit of fun.'

'Who's this Russian then?' Arnold asked.

'He's a prodigy pianist. Come over with lots of hype. We haven't done any rehearsals with him yet so God knows what he's like.'

'He's supposed to be really ace.'

'He'd better be,' said John Pike. 'All the publicity he's got.'

'Yes, they make out he's carrying the orchestra – that brochure they put out, it more or less says, "Come and listen to Boris Whatshisname-ski accompanied by a rubbish orchestra but he's worth your while." Did you read it?' Nutty was full of indignation. 'All pictures of him and his retinue and none of us at all!'

'He didn't even come in the coach, did he? He has his own car,' Jodie put in.

'What, drives it?'

'No, he's not old enough. His minders drive it – his mum and dad, or whatever. Hatchet-faced woman, haven't you seen her? And her husband and another fellow, youngish, face like a ferret.'

'She's not old enough to be his mother,' Jodie said.

'She and her husband are his managers,' John Pike said. 'He's their bread and butter. No wonder they guard him like the crown jewels.'

'Sounds as if he could do with a bit of light relief,' Christian said. 'We'll indoctrinate him with our low standards.'

'Oh, hark at you! The most dedicated of the lot!' Jodie crowed.

Christian went slightly pink.

John Pike said, 'Lay off! He can't help it. His father's a General.'

'My father's a greengrocer and I've got very high standards,' said Nutty loftily.

'My father's a VAT man.' Hoomey looked as if this explained everything.

46

'Mine's a burglar,' said Arnold.

They all looked awed.

'You mean, he makes a living at it?'

'Yeah. But he's abroad just now, in Spain.'

'Crime *does* pay?'

'On and off. Mostly off.' Arnold had discovered this for himself. To be successful one needed brains, just like being a General. Life had its patterns.

This interesting conversation was broken up by the intrusion of Mrs Knox once more. They had been so taken up with yakking that they had forgotten to hide Arnold yet again. He tried to fade behind the door, but her eyes behind their large owlish glasses seemed to pierce like lasers. However she had stopped counting beds and was introducing the Russian boy.

'This is Boris Khobotov, who is going to stay with you. I want you to make quite sure he isn't left out of things.' She beamed a laser smile at Boris and added to Christian quietly, 'He seems like a nervous wreck to me. You must do your best. Let me know if you can't cope. I'll be keeping an eye on you.'

Arnold thought, 'That's all we need! Special attention!'

Boris was staggering beneath an enormous suitcase. Christian took it off him with a Christian smile and laid it on the best of the four beds with a flourish of his arm to indicate that this was Boris's place. Then, pointing to each of them in turn, he said their names, and they all shook hands. As Mrs Knox was still hovering in the doorway, Arnold was David Smith again.

Boris was a pale gangling lad of about sixteen, all wrists and Adam's apple. He had huge dark eyes in a gaunt white face and lank black hair that fell like a horse's forelock over his brainy brow. His smile was flickering, nervous, his large hands damp with sweat. He murmured polite (presumably) Russian which was incomprehensible.

Mrs Knox departed and an embarrassed silence fell on the company. Nutty and Jodie melted back to their own room. Christian and John Pike made a show of unpacking their things and Christian got out his clarinet and played a few random twiddles. Boris undid the enormous suitcase and opened the wardrobe door. He hung all his clothes on hangers and started to line up about ten pairs of shoes on the wardrobe floor where Arnold was going to sleep. Arnold sat miserably watching him. Life was getting complicated.

'What am I going to do?' he appealed.

'Oh, don't worry. We'll sort it out later. I'm just hoping David Smith is keeping out of the limelight, wherever he is.'

It was a bit of a lark to the others, Arnold

could see. Life and death to him – although death seemed to have receded a bit. They had to go down for a talk in the hall, about the two weeks ahead of them, and then they were shown a film so boring (blokes in silk stockings singing) that Arnold dozed off and fell off his chair. John Pike caught him just before he crashed to the floor where no doubt Mrs Knox's lasers would have caught up with him. At supper the extra place was laid already, and Arnold got down to an enormous meal of soup, roast beef and all the trimmings, fruit salad and coffee. When they were all finished Mr Harlech, the general manager of the orchestra and boss organizer, spoke to them briefly.

'Tomorrow after breakfast you will all assemble in the ballroom with your instruments for our first rehearsal. Try to get a good sleep tonight – some of us will be round the dormitories after lights out to make sure you're not messing about. This isn't just a holiday and a joke, remember – you're here to do a job. Enjoy yourselves by all means, but show you are worthy of having been chosen by having a responsible attitude. I know you won't let me down.'

'Huh,' breathed Nutty. 'I hope you're right, mate.'

'Just before you go!' Mr Harlech raised his voice as Mrs Knox spoke anxiously in his ear.

He held up his hand for silence. 'Can David Smith just come and see Mrs Knox before he goes upstairs. Thank you!'

Arnold froze in his seat. Christian nudged him urgently to his feet.

'Not you, twit! The real one. It's the wardrobe for you, quick sharp.'

They raced up the baronial stairs towards the third floor.

'She'll come looking,' Jodie panted.

'Of course. But we'll have time to hide him.'

'Let us know what happens!' Jodie and Nutty departed for the female dormitories and the boys regained their room. A rather bewildered Boris followed them and watched as they scooped his neat rows of shoes into a heap at one end of the wardrobe and stuffed Arnold inside. John Pike shut the door on him.

The experience – of hiding while Authority searched nearby – was not entirely foreign to Arnold. All the same he felt unaccountably more nervous this time than he ever had before. The wardrobe was as dark as a tomb and smelled strongly of age, damp and mothballs. He could hear quite plainly everything going on in the room. In no time at all he heard Mrs Knox's voice.

'Can you explain to me why we have two David Smiths in our company? Where's that boy who was in here before supper? The one with hair like bristles who scowled all the time.'

'I don't know, Mrs Knox. He's not a friend of ours. He just came in, looking for a bed, I think.'

'But you said he was David Smith. And there's already a David Smith at the other end of the corridor.'

'I thought he said he was David Smith.'

'Who was he then?'

'I don't know.'

'Was he at supper?'

'Yes. He sat near us.'

'Did he come upstairs with you after supper?'

'I don't know where he went after supper.'

'I can't make it out. If you see him again, will you send him to me? I need to get this straight. We seem to have an extra person.'

There was a long pause. Arnold could see them all standing looking innocent and responsible. For a General's son, Christian was a great liar.

In a less irritable tone of voice Mrs Knox then said, 'And Boris – is everything going all right with Boris? He looks a little bewildered.'

Not surprising, Arnold thought. Probably wondering about his shoes.

'Everything all right, Boris?'

Boris said something which probably meant: 'No. There's something nasty in the wardrobe and they've messed up my shoes,' but Mrs Knox merely replied, 'I'm sure you'll be very happy here, Boris. We all want you to have a good time, to enjoy yourself.'

Another pause, then, rather doubtfully, 'All right then. If you see that boy again, will you let me know? Settle down straight away, will you? Boris needs his rest.'

'Yes, Mrs Knox.'

She departed. Christian opened the door but wouldn't let Arnold out. 'She might come back. Just stay there.'

'You were bloomin' good,' Arnold said.

'I don't like telling lies,' Christian said gloomily.

'It's all in a good cause,' said Hoomey cheerfully.

'Not serious lies,' John Pike said, seeming to understand Christian's point of view, which Arnold didn't. 'You've forgotten what we're hiding Arnold – Ron – for. Someone tried to murder him. We're supposed to be protecting him.'

Arnold nearly said, 'Your father would be proud of you,' but didn't.

'True. We were careless in the first place, letting her see him. If we're going through with it, we've got to be far more careful. It could get serious.'

'It doesn't help having Boris. She'll be popping in to see him all the time.'

'What can we say to him?'

Boris was sitting on his bed looking pole-axed by what was going on.

Christian did a mime of hiding Arnold, putting his fingers to his lips and shaking his head, laughing – trying to convey a joke, a secret – all obviously in vain. Boris looked as if he was going to burst into tears.

'We'll have to get a Russian dictionary.'

It had been a long day. Christian yawned suddenly and groaned. 'Let's sleep on it. I've had enough.'

They threw some spare blankets at Arnold, made reassuring noises at Boris, undressed and got into bed. Boris slowly followed suit. Quite shortly, long relaxed breathing told Arnold he was alone in consciousness, washed up on a pile of shoes in the bottom of a wardrobe, with not a lot to look forward to. He went to sleep just two hours before it was time to get up again.

CHAPTER FOUR

Arnold, hungry as he was the next morning, could see that there was no way he could go down to breakfast. Mrs Knox's gimlet eyes were now alert for the boy with hair like bristles. David Smith had been heard complaining about some gink playing tricks on him.

'You'll actually be safest in the orchestra with us,' Christian decided. 'Sit at the back with the percussion – nobody knows who's hitting what up there. Take a book to read. The only danger will be dying of boredom.'

Arnold didn't read books. Doing nothing was quite attractive to him. Missing breakfast not so.

'We'll bring you some up, don't worry. Between us we'll grab a feast. Then we'll smuggle you out to the ballroom in the crowd and you'll be OK.'

They all did another pantomime for the benefit of the fazed Boris, to indicate secrecy, big joke, say nothing, hush, ha-ha, and departed for breakfast leaving Arnold sitting sulkily in the bottom of his wardrobe. After the stampede downstairs all was peace and quiet, the only sound the raucous calling of the big black birds that freewheeled down the valley on the back of a brisk westerly wind. The rain seemed to have stopped. Arnold risked having a look out of the window, and was awed by the grandeur of the mountains that hemmed in the valley, range upon range in fading tones of bruised grey-violet, no less impressive on further contemplation than they were at first sight. Some people, he knew, sought them for pleasure. His eyes widened at the thought. The wardrobe seemed far friendlier by contrast. He sat patiently, picking at the scabs on his neck.

The boys came back with, between them, six rolls with bacon rashers inside and two cups of tea.

'Try sticking a cup of tea up your jumper and running upstairs,' John Pike said. 'It's painful.'

'It's only half a cup,' Arnold complained.

'Count yourself lucky! I'll wring out my shirt if you want some more.'

Boris handed over a bacon roll with a shy smile. He seemed to have got the gist of the game. He seemed more relaxed and looked slightly less zombied than he had the night before.

'He might be human after all,' John Pike said.

'He's said to be a genius,' Hoomey said. 'It must make you a bit funny.'

'You're a bit funny and you're no genius.'

'I didn't say it worked that way round.'

Hoomey was obviously used to being sat on. It didn't seem to depress him at all. They had got used to talking about Boris while nodding and smiling at him and he seemed to enjoy their company. He was rather like a large dog in the room, Arnold thought, wagging his tail.

'Can I come out now?' Arnold asked.

'Yeah, we're off to the ballroom. Get your violin case and keep your head down. Hoomey can go on ahead and see if old gimlet-eyes is on the war-path. She was looking around at breakfast. Good thing you didn't appear.'

Arnold felt distinctly nervous emerging. Luckily everyone was making the same exit and there was quite a crowd. Jodie and Nutty joined them at the top of the stairs.

'We've got news for you,' Nutty said darkly.

'What's that?'

'When we got back upstairs after breakfast Mrs Knox was on the landing, and she was saying to old Harlech, "That extra boy seems to have disappeared. But just to make sure, I'll do a thorough tour of all the dormitories tonight, look under the beds and in all the wardrobes. It's probably a dare, a lark of some sort, but we really can't have this sort of thing." '

Her mimicry was excellent. Arnold's heart, already at half-mast, plummeted.

Christian only grinned. 'Lucky you heard!'

'What'll I do?'

'You'll have to sleep on the hillside, old matey, like a proper Highlander.' Then, seriously, seeing Arnold's face, 'Don't be daft. We'll think of something. She'll never search the whole bally place – take her all night.'

But the problems of the present moment were too tricky to take on future problems as well. Hoomey came panting back, pink with excitement.

'She's standing at the door, watching everyone go out!'

Christian only hesitated a moment. Then, at the bottom of the stairs, he took Arnold's elbow and propelled him not across the hall towards the main door but down behind the tables and out through the door to the kitchen. It was neatly and swiftly done. They went down a short corridor and into a large kitchen where several stout ladies were stacking dishes, scraping frying-pans, drinking tea, joking and gossiping. None of them took any notice. Christian and Arnold went out of the nearest door into the yard and rejoined the crowd. Arnold reckoned Christian had inherited the General's genes.

'Clever!' said John Pike.

Boris grinned. He seemed to have cottoned on. When they went into the ballroom he gestured to the open lid of the big concert grand piano that stood there, gestured to Arnold that he get inside, and pretended to close the lid. They all laughed.

'He's not a bad cheese,' John Pike said.

'He's a complication, all the same,' Christian said, his General's genes talking.

The ballroom was every bit as weird as John Pike had predicted. It was a large hall with a high, arching timber roof, and from all the roof beams and the top half of the walls serried ranks of antlers of all shapes and sizes were locked in a great frieze of dead bone. Here and there a whole stuffed head stared with glassy eyes upon the alien scene, bearing a majestic canopy of antlers. On many of the white gleaming skulls little brass plates inscribed the date of death and by whom the beasts were shot: mostly titled gentlemen and a fair sprinkling of royalty. Some of the more sensitive vegetarians reeled wanly at the sight. It was bestial or noble, according to one's attitude, impressive to all.

'It used to be the ballroom for the clan's festivities,' the eager Mr Harlech was lecturing. 'What a sight it must have been! Can you imagine it? What ghosts must lurk around here!'

The members of the orchestra took their places

with a terrific crashing and scraping of chairs and music stands and much chatter. Jodie departed to the front line of violins and Christian somewhere to the middle back where everyone seemed to have some sort of pipe. Brass instruments ranged behind them. Arnold was shepherded by John Pike to his enormous array of drums which were lined up at the back, on the left. The rows being tiered, and the drums on the top, Arnold felt he would be terribly exposed, but once he had sat down, legs dangling, he realized that he was completely hidden from the front behind the row of bodies before him. If he really wanted to hide there were caves beneath him formed by the floors of the tiered seating. Behind him again, he noticed a small exit door. Self preservation had long ago accustomed him to taking in escape routes. Nothing much had changed in his life, after all.

Hoomey, with his triangle, took an amiable seat beside him.

'I hardly ever have to play,' he said. 'And when I do, Nutty kicks me a minute or two beforehand. So I don't have to worry too much.'

Arnold looked at the little silver triangle dubiously.

'Hardly worth it, is it?'

'It doesn't make much noise, no. Not like Nutty's stuff. If she gets it wrong everyone knows.'

Nutty stood staunchly above them setting her vast cymbals into their stand. She stood four-square, a hunk of a girl, and Arnold could just picture her muscled arms holding the brass discs aloft waiting for the moment of blast-off. He wouldn't mind that sort of a job. He had a nervous admiration for this apparently fearless girl. He had fallen in with a useful lot, all in all, with the General's son to take command. Christian would find him a good berth for the night, he decided. He would trust in his judgement.

John Pike dropped a drum-cover over his head. 'No-one would ever know.'

He lifted it up again, grinning. 'Just for emergencies. If Fort Knox comes counting. I'll make sure you disappear.'

He started tuning his drums, and the quiet thunder in Arnold's ear made him realize he certainly wouldn't be nodding off. He prepared for a long morning.

The conductor was an enthusiastic young man with long yellow hair called Andrew Carruthers. Hoomey told Arnold he was very short-sighted and couldn't see any of them individually, so not to worry. 'He knows who's playing, of course, and can talk in the right direction, but he doesn't know anybody's names, save a few of the leaders.'

During the course of the rehearsal Arnold discovered that his minders were quite important people. Jodie seemed to be boss of the violins and Christian did quite a lot of piping on his own, with very impressive twiddling, while the orchestra kept softly in the background. John Pike made an equally impressive noise, bending reverently over his array of drums, dodging from one to another and twiddling with their buttons between times. Nutty, after fidgeting impatiently in her seat for half the morning, eventually rose to take up her cymbals, standing like Rule Britannia awaiting her cue. The music grew louder and louder and when everyone was piping, scraping and blowing at the very limit – it seemed to Arnold – of their endurance it was all topped off by Nutty crashing her cymbals together like God Almighty, her face crimson with excitement. Hoomey by contrast got up and tinkled his triangle once or twice but to very little effect. In one of the lulls Arnold asked him why he did it, it was so boring, but Hoomey smiled and said, 'It's all right. Why not?' to which Arnold had no reply. He could see why Nutty did it – what power! – but the other players, like Jodie and Christian, appeared to be doing something very clever which no doubt involved many hours of hard work – not an attractive proposition to Arnold.

After a couple of hours Mr Carruthers said there would be a break for refreshments. 'Then we'll try out the piano concerto with our Russian friend.'

The Russian friend seemed to have gone to sleep in a sagging armchair under the gaze of a dead stag.

The refreshments arrived and were devoured, Arnold joining the throng and eating busily, aware that meals were going to be hard to come by in the immediate future. Boris woke up and the grand piano was manoeuvered across the floor to its place beside the conductor, and everyone drifted back to their places. Boris sat on his stool and twiddled it down to a comfortable level while Mr Carruthers addressed the orchestra.

'Boris understands no English at all, as you are probably aware. This might lead to a few problems, but we'll just have to keep our fingers crossed all will go well. Not while we're playing, of course.' Everyone laughed politely at the joke. 'Boris knows this Grieg concerto very well – probably, I fear, a lot better than we do, so our job will be to accord him an accompaniment to the very best of our ability. I stress this because, as I think you understand, this young man is phenomenally talented and we are extremely lucky to have him on this tour. I think our audiences next week will be much attracted by his appearance as soloist. Let us not delude ourselves that they will all be coming just to hear us! On the other hand, we can do our cause a great deal of good if we support him, each one of us, with our very best efforts. It is a great opportunity for us and one we would be very foolish to waste. So your best attention, please!'

He tapped imperiously on his music stand and straightened up. He then directed his newly officious gaze straight in Arnold's direction and gave him a nod. Arnold nearly jumped out of his skin as a drumroll so loud from right beside his left ear nearly threw him down amongst the violins. John Pike's very best efforts were then taken up by Boris crashing his large hands down on the keyboard and making an equally loud noise. This fortunately allowed John Pike to fade away, and Jodie and Co came sweeping in to add to the racket, bows waving like saplings in a breeze. Arnold had never heard such a row. So much for reading a book or dozing off! He had always thought this classy sort of music was quiet and civilized. By the end of it, John Pike's best efforts had pulverized him. He felt as glassy-eyed as the dead stags.

Boris had worked very hard. When it was finished the whole orchestra clapped him and shouted, 'Bravo, Boris!' with obviously spontaneous enthusiasm. Boris's wide Mongolian face turned pink as Mr Carruthers shook him by the hand. Even Arnold could appreciate that their Boris was quite something.

For the rest of the morning they worked on various bits with lots of stopping and starting and eventually they were dismissed to go back for lunch. Christian weaved his way between the music stands and stood looking down on the shrinking Arnold.

'It'll be dangerous, the dining-room. I think you ought to stay here for now, and we'll bring you some dinner out. I was thinking, actually, this would be a pretty safe place tonight, while Fort Knox is on the prowl.'

'What, here?'

'More comfortable than the wardrobe. A whole hall to yourself.'

Arnold didn't like to elaborate on his instinctive dislike of the idea. He couldn't admit what a chicken he was when it came to dark and lonely places. Even in daylight, when everyone had departed, the hall gave him the creeps with its dado of death. So what if it was a place of pageant for celebrating clans? Celebrating what? A massacre up the glen, no doubt. The decorations in the big house consisted mainly of crossed swords, clubs and sundry skull-cleavers. One could get killed in these wild and lonely places without anyone knowing at all. Who was going to search a million square miles of wet heather for a Barking boy not strictly known to exist?

'Oh, come off it, Ron,' Nutty said loftily when she appeared with his dinner (stew and veg in a plastic bag, not a pretty sight) and he voiced his fears. (She was only a girl, after all.) 'Chris is right – you're absolutely safe out here. You can come back tomorrow and sleep in the wardrobe again. It's a great lark, after all. There's a spare bed in our room. We ought to find you a wig and you can change into a girl.'

She was full of ideas.

She peered into the caverns under the wooden staging. 'You could sleep an army under here and no-one'd see. We'll make you really comfortable. Blankets and a torch and some grub, and you can have my personal stereo, if you like. John Pike noticed there's a fire-escape on the end wall of the house and the door goes out from the end of the corridor right next to their room. That could be jolly useful. The door's locked but the key's still in.'

She could talk the hind legs off a donkey. Arnold ate his stew with the spoon she provided. When she had gone he realized that the gloss had gone off the whole adventure. Being on his own, even if safe, was no fun, and the coming ordeal of the night alone with two thousand skulls began to weigh him down.

CHAPTER FIVE

Jodie and Nutty collected some spare blankets and pillows for Arnold (women's work), and took them along to the boys to take out to the hall (man's work).

'Wait till it gets dark,' Jodie suggested.

'It doesn't get dark up here,' Christian said. 'Haven't you noticed?'

'Good point.'

'Pike and I'll go out down the fire-escape when it looks quiet. We'll take Arnold's supper out at the same time. Lie low tonight, and tomorrow he can come back.'

'Is someone really trying to murder him?' John Pike asked Jodie. 'Or is it just some daft scheme you're playing at?'

'I saw the motorbike attack him. That was real all right. And when he saw the body – that's when I met him—'

She explained about Arnold's bursting out of the bushes on the night of the party, and the body that might have been a deck-chair.

'He said he saw it close to, and it *was* a body. He went and blabbed about it at the party, so we thought the murderer heard him and tried to stop him before he spread the news around.' She shrugged; it seemed rather far away now. In the daylight, with the adults all proving themselves God-fearing, smiling, kindly people whose only wish was that they should all be happy musicians, the threats of the night before last seemed to have lost their impact.

'All the same, quite a few of the people at that party are here in this house now. So if what he says is all true . . . ' John Pike looked quite excited at the thought.

'He didn't make up those holes in his neck,' Jodie said. 'They weren't there when I spoke to him the first time.'

'You'd need to find the body, to make anyone believe his story,' Christian decided.

'I could ring home, and see if there's any news about it – how about that?' Jodie appealed.

'Yeah, but do we really want to know?' Nutty said. 'It's quite fun as it is, but if it's real – I mean, if there really is a murderer here, that's not a lot of fun, is it?'

'No,' said Hoomey. 'And nobody seems to have missed the body. If he was supposed to be with the orchestra, there's nobody missing, is there?'

'Not that I've heard of.'

'We'll play it by ear,' Christian decided. 'See what happens.'

It was very hard to explain to Boris what was going on. He was mystified by the whole Arnold thing, and had rearranged his shoes in the wardrobe. He smiled, whatever they said to him. After hearing him play, they had all decided that yes, he was a genius. Also yes, he was a bit of a weirdo. He had practised in the hall all afternoon with his minders (and Arnold, had he but known it, hiding under the seating platforms, thinking about food) and had been obviously pleased to shake them off afterwards and come back to the dormitory. His managers occupied the best room on the floor below, immediately under the one Christian had appropriated, and still apparently wanted Boris to stay with them. Boris conveyed this by mime, making disliking faces when the female Russian had come up to argue with him. She had a face like a nutcracker, with outlying nose and chin, and sharp black eyes.

'No wonder he prefers it here,' Nutty remarked. She wasn't a looking-after sort of woman, it was obvious.

When she had gone Boris gave a thumbs-up sign.

Nutty had a feeling she could quite easily fall for Boris. Unluckily boys fell for the Jodies of this world, and Nutty had to grind them down by perseverance. She decided to acquire a Russian dictionary and get started. While she was visiting every room along the corridor with a cry of, 'Anyone learn Russian here?' Christian and John Pike set off to take provisions to Arnold in the ballroom.

It was nine o'clock and only slightly dusky. The evening was cool and damp and the far mountains were lost in a sunshot haze where the clouds had momentarily parted to allow a few moments of impressive sunset. A golden glow spread eerily over the wide valley. The boys paused on the top of the fire escape, impressed by the grandeur of the scene. The ballroom of stags' antlers seemed all of a piece seen in its wild setting, its back to the turbulent river.

They had to cross the yard where the coaches and several cars were parked. The ballroom lay on the far side in a grove of pine trees. They got down the iron staircase and were crossing the yard when a tractor approached from over the bridge, its headlights swinging across the yard as it turned into one of the barns. They froze behind a convenient car, bobbing their heads down as the light flared.

In that moment Christian saw, lying across the car's dashboard, a pair of fur gloves. On the tip of each finger was a claw. On any other occasion he would have seen them for joke gloves, frighteners, but he knew instantly that he was looking at the gloves that Arnold had felt round his neck. He grabbed John Pike's arm.

'Look!'

But the tractor headlights had gone. Dazzled, John Pike could only see the vague shape of the gloves Christian was pointing at.

'The claws that strangled him—!'

But they couldn't stand around in the open. They doubled up and sped for the shelter of the pine trees. Christian jerked out what he had seen.

'Whose car is it?' John Pike peered back across the yard.

'God knows. We'll get its number as we go back. It's that black one, a Citroen, I think.'

'Don't tell Arnold!'

Christian could see John Pike's point. As they opened the door into the ballroom they were both struck by a distinctly spooky atmosphere. In the half-light the white skulls seemed to give off a phosphorescent sheen, glimmering in the high arches of the ancient roof. Looking up in awe, they felt as if the empty eye-sockets had been filled again with the vengeful eyes of two thousand slaughtered beasts. A musky damp smell permeated the place, like old foxes and wet leaves, and the river could be heard booming over the rocks two hundred metres away, swollen by the rain.

They shut the door behind them with what they hoped was a cheerful crash and shouted for Arnold. He emerged from the back of the stage eagerly.

'What's for supper then?'

They had managed to bring a plate this time and their scavengings looked quite attractive: several slices of ham, six large potatoes, two hard-boiled eggs, three tomatoes and a wedge of cucumber slices. While Arnold ate, apparently quite cheerful, Christian and John Pike were traumatized by the incident of the gloves. Suddenly the great lark they had been enjoying had turned into the serious thing Jodie had told them it was. They neither of them had really believed it. Now they did. The shock was considerable.

'Everything all right?' Arnold noticed their reticence.

'Yes, fine . . . we'd better get back, before we're found missing.'

Christian hesitated. He knew he wouldn't want to spend a night alone in this morgue, even without a murderer after him.

'We'll come in the morning. I wouldn't – I wouldn't leave here until we come. Not off your own bat, I mean.'

'OK, boss.' Arnold grinned.

They retreated, leaving Arnold still scoffing. John Pike shut the door firmly behind them and they stood in the porch, looking across the yard. Nothing moved. The great fortified manor house with its grim stone front glowered before them, the black hillside pressing down behind. A few stars glimmered faintly in the pale sky.

They dodged back between the cars. Christian took the number of the car with the gloves on the dashboard, although it was now impossible to make them out. It was quite a relief to get back up the iron staircase and into the racket of the dormitory floor. Nutty was returning triumphantly waving a Russian dictionary; Jodie was trying out Christian's clarinet.

'Fort Knox is on her way!' Hoomey had been keeping look-out.

'Just in time!'

The girls scattered for home.

At one of the windows a watcher smiled grimly. In his pocket he had a length of wiring flex. Strangling was simple and quiet, with luck, and this time he would make no mistake. A body dumped in a patch of bracken on the hillside would certainly never be found. With the meddling boy gone, no-one could ever prove there had ever been another body, or even, come to that, a meddling boy. Tonight he would disappear for good.

CHAPTER SIX

After he had finished his dinner, Arnold gathered up the bedding and dragged it down to his hidey-hole under the orchestra platform. It was quite roomy under the back row. He laid out the blankets and pillow, and realized that he felt not the slightest bit sleepy. It was dark in the hall but his new friends had given him a good torch. He wandered round and lay in the sagging armchair for a bit: it was more comfortable than the floor. On a small table nearby several leaflets were scattered, mostly to do with the Youth Orchestra and its visit.

Arnold leafed through them idly, shining the torch on the photos to see if he could recognize his friends. There was a large photo of Boris sitting at a piano and, opposite, a photo of a man in evening dress. The face looked familiar. Underneath, it said he was Igor Turkin, manager to Boris Khobotov.

Arnold frowned. It wasn't the man Boris was travelling with now. No sign of Nutcracker face either. But why did the face of Igor Turkin seem familiar?

Arnold stared at it in the torchlight, with that tantalizing feeling of knowing he had seen it before. At the party? Something to do with the party . . . no, in the water . . . it was the face of the body. *The dead body!*

Arnold could not help a yelp escaping him. Given that the Igor of the photo was dry, combed and smiling, and the face Arnold had seen was dead and slimy, there was no mistaking in Arnold's mind that it was the same man. Boris's manager! So Boris was in the conspiracy that he seemed to have walked into! And who was the present manager? Arnold could recall the wife's face, all jutting jaw and straight, unlovely hair, and young Ferretface, whose job seemed to be to drive the Russians' car, but the third man had a less obtrusive presence than his two friends. Arnold remembered a bland face; no features came to mind. To the best of his knowledge, nobody had mentioned the missing Igor, no-one had enquired as to why Boris's manager had changed his face. True, Boris appeared to be a nervous wreck, but that was because he was a genius. Or was it because he knew? Knew what? Arnold realized he didn't know either.

Whether Igor fell in or was pushed? Had he been murdered, or merely careless?

Arnold lay back in his armchair, his mind reeling with too much conjecture. Whatever Igor's fate, there was definitely a murderer around, so it seemed reasonable to assume he had done for Igor. Arnold had stumbled upon the body and was now in danger of being erased himself.

Arnold groped his way rapidly back to the comfort of his cave and got under the blankets. He had been unhappy in the wardrobe last night but was now desperate to be back in its dark embrace, listening to the comforting snuffles, snorts and deep breathing of his companions. In here there was only the distant murmur of the river and the sighing of the wind in the pine trees. No sound of a living creature, only the silence of the long-dead stags whose great antlers closed like a forest all round him, two thousand of them at bay against their killers.

Arnold knew what they felt like.

Whether he dozed off or not he did not know, but it seemed that time had passed; the floor was hard, the hall was dark, and there was a noise at the far end by the door which sounded like a handle being turned. Arnold lifted his head off the pillow. There came a gentle creaking, as of the heavy door moving, and a squeaking of a floorboard. No more.

Arnold lay back, clammy with fright. He could hear his heart hammering, as if it was in his head, not his chest. Of course, Boris knew he was in the ballroom and he had told his murdering minders . . . Fort Knox finding him in the wardrobe would be nothing compared with what he faced now.

He lay still, holding his breath to try and catch the smallest sound. His first panic had been overtaken by a rather familiar determination in the face of danger. He would have to rely on his wits now, if this was a man intending to kill him.

The ancient wooden floor sighed to the footsteps passing. A faint creak . . . there was no doubt someone was in the room. A ray of torchlight flickered momentarily on a row of white skulls and faded. Now Arnold could hear the footsteps approaching. He held his breath. If the torch came looking under the staging, he would be lost.

He pulled the blanket right over him and held up a corner to see through. In the dim light – his eyes becoming accustomed – he saw a pair of legs walking past, very slowly. The torchlight was searching the stacked chairs, screens and various rubbish that lined the far wall. Arnold could see no higher than the man's behind.

Opposite Arnold was the small Exit door that let out at the back of the hall. He knew it was unlocked. If the intruder did not give up but came searching more thoroughly, Arnold decided to make a bolt for it. He stood far more chance out in the open, could run like a hare if his life depended on it. The legs disappeared out of vision, returning to the front of the orchestra stand. Arnold dithered as to whether to go or not. But betted on the intruder departing, having found nothing. Wrongly, as it turned out.

The man went up to the top of the hall again and there was a long and wracking silence. Then the footsteps came again over the creaking floor, round the back of the staging. This time the torch was turned inward.

Arnold ran. The man was still out of his vision, round the curve of the staging, and Arnold, doubled up, went silently, hoping to get to the door unseen. But as he straightened up to open the door, a board creaked beneath his foot. The torch flew in his direction, pinning him in its bright light.

He wrenched at the door handle and flung himself through the door. The man came after him. Instead of running straight, Arnold right-angled and ran down the back wall to the corner, then launched off among the pine trees in the direction of the river. One instinct told him to make for the house, but another told him to keep his new friends out of trouble if possible. He was adept at eluding capture but always across friendly tarmac: the dark and hostile hillside before him was something else. He plunged down, leaping and scrambling through the thick heather roots, making for the sound of the river. It gave a sense of direction, although it wasn't a practical proposition. Better would be to head up the valley and make for the track that led away, following the river, towards the far mountains: they had seen that clearly from their bedroom window. He would try and lose his murderer, and then make up the valley to try and find somewhere to lie low until morning.

The torchlight caught him, lost him as he leapt sideways and fell in landing. The uneven ground had dropped him in a nice hole. Taking advantage, he turned and crawled and wriggled back in the opposite direction, keeping his head down, following an animal track. The man ran to the spot where the light had picked him out and stood there, flashing the torch all round. Arnold froze to the ground.

His pursuer was about five metres away. Arnold buried his face into the earth and waited. The torchlight flickered all round like a will-o'-the-wisp over the dank heather. Arnold could hear the man's heavy, angry breathing and the squelching of his feet as he moved direction. The man knew he was there and persisted, searching, but when he decided to stamp his way around the area to flush Arnold out, he fortunately chose the down-river direction, and turned his back for a few moments. Arnold took the opportunity to wriggle a little further. It was imperative to make no noise. Fortunately the river rolling over loose rocks made a grumbling, gravelling noise which covered up the rustling of his snakelike progress. He put several more metres between himself and the searcher before the torch turned back uphill in his direction.

He lay still again, face down. It was only chance that would see him through. The man stamped backwards and forwards, at one point coming to within an arm's length. His stamping foot flicked wet earth in Arnold's face. Arnold stopped breathing; his pulse thumped so loud it seemed to fill the night. But his luck held. Within centimetres of him, the man swore and muttered and turned away. The torchlight went on down to the river and Arnold heard cursing and crashings, but gradually the sounds of pursuit receded.

Arnold crawled on along a sketchy tunnel made by animals, making uphill for the track which he knew led away from the big house up the valley. He thought, if he made back to the house, the man would be lying in wait for him and in the other direction lay safety. If he lifted his head he could see the lights of the old fortified manor-house some eight hundred metres away, looking very inviting, safe and cosy. Fort Knox would be peanuts beside the hunter that was searching for him at the moment. But it would be suicide to go back. He had no alternative.

He laid up for about half an hour, cold, wet and shivering. A half moon came out from behind the clouds and lit up the silent valley and let loose a few glittering stars to wink at him from above the fell tops. Nothing moved.

Very carefully Arnold crept to his feet and, hunching down, started to move up the valley. All was quiet. Gradually he straightened up, moving fast, but there was no pursuit. He had no idea what lay up the valley but it must be better than what lay in wait in the other direction.

'He's not there!'

Jodie came back to the boys' room after breakfast, still with Arnold's filched portion in the capacious 'hand-warmer' pocket of her sweatshirt. She looked eight months pregnant.

'Not a sign of him. His bed's all rumpled and – what was odd – the back door was open.'

'Perhaps he's just gone down to the river to wash,' Hoomey suggested.

'Out of character,' said Nutty. 'Wash! Would you?'

It was raining again. They knew she was right.

'Something's wrong. He wouldn't have moved otherwise,' Christian said.

'Perhaps Claws has got him?'

Hoomey looked pale. The story of the furry gloves in the car had terrified him. They had discovered that the car was the one used by Boris's keepers. With this disturbing information to hand, Nutty had prepared to question Boris about the dead body, but had not got him to comprehend that *oobivat*, according to her dictionary, meant murder. Instead of turning pale and fleeing the room he had looked bemused. *Abazoor* for lampshade he had cottoned on to, but Nutty had only experimented with lampshade because it was easy, not because she wanted to talk about lampshades. Russian was not a user-friendly language, she had quickly discovered, not even having a comprehensible alphabet. To fall in love appeared to be *vlyooblyatsya*; sweetheart was *vaz-lyooblyen-nay*. Even if she wanted to call Boris her sweetheart, by the time she had got her tongue round *vaz-lyooblyen-nay* his concentration would have worn off.

'If Claws has got him,' Jodie said, 'he'd only have to drag his body out in the heather somewhere and no-one would ever find him. Suppose he doesn't turn up? We'll have to tell someone.'

'They'll think we're spoofing. There's no proof he exists,' John Pike pointed out. 'Not after last night when the count was all correct. I heard Fort Knox saying she must have made a mistake.'

'No proof of a body in the first place either,' Jodie added. 'He swore it was, but I couldn't be sure. I *am* sure someone's trying to murder him though.'

'Murder who? they'll say. It's all terribly flimsy when you think it through,' Christian said. 'This murderer, if he exists, has got everything on his side.'

'So what do we do if Arnold doesn't turn up?' Jodie asked. 'Shop the Russians?'

'On the evidence of the gloves? Without Arnold and the holes in his neck, there's no evidence there either. Boris doesn't look like a crook to me.'

Boris was smiling amiably all the time this conversation was going on, presumably thinking it was all about music.

'It's not Boris. It's his minders. I think Claws is that ferret-faced one,' Nutty declared.

'We'll see what happens this morning. Arnold'll probably turn up. If not—' Christian shrugged. He had meant to get some practice in before the orchestral rehearsal, but now it was too late. They were playing their first concert in the afternoon, leaving by coach for a community hall some twenty miles away, and there were a few sections he was still not truly confident about. Christian took his music seriously, and this lark with Arnold, a good wheeze at the beginning, was fast getting too complicated.

They went out to the ballroom with the crowd at the appointed time: still no sign of Arnold. The rehearsal got under way and they played the music they had to present in the afternoon. Nutty had lots of cymbal crashes at the climax of her favourite piece; Hoomey had some delicate triangle work to perfect and Jodie and Christian each had lots of solos. Between them their minds were fully occupied. In the break for elevenses talk was all of tempo, semi-quavers and easily-forgotten repeat signs rather than claws, crooks and stiffs.

When John Pike went back to his timpani he found Arnold sitting under his drum-cover.

'Blimey, where've you sprung from?'

Arnold was wet through, as white as a ghost and shivering with cold.

'He tried to wipe me out last night! I'm not leaving you lot again!'

'Who did? Who is it?'

'How can I tell, in the dark? Chased me all down to the river.'

'How did he know you were there?'

'You tell me. Who knew where I was?'

Boris, thought John Pike, but didn't say.

'I found out – the body – who the body is, was,' said Arnold.

The conductor rapped for attention and raised his baton to start. Arnold bobbed down. John Pike dropped his drumsticks and as the piece opened with a drum-roll nothing happened.

'Mr Pike?' queried the conductor.

'Sorry, sir!'

Christian looked behind, amused, and saw Arnold's face disappearing round the side of the bass drum.

John Pike started and Christian then missed his cue, shell-shocked by seeing Arnold, and they started for the third time.

Arnold cowered down, waiting for the morning to finish. It seemed long and he felt frazzled, but the knowledge that he was back with his keepers gave him a great sense of security. In his heart he knew that this sense was quite false, for the murderer was persistent, coldblooded and undoubtedly close at hand. But Arnold had faith in numbers: to keep close . . . the killer could hardly do away with all six of them? Fort Knox would surely then find her numbers amiss.

When the morning was over at last, they took Arnold back to the dormitory in the crowd. There, sitting on the bed, wrapped in an eider-down, Arnold told them what had happened the night before.

'I found an old house up the valley and I stayed

there and in the morning when it got light I started walking back. I met some blokes – gamekeepers – I told 'em I'd got lost and they said I was stupid but they didn't ask any questions. But look—'

Arnold groped in his jeans pocket and pulled out the leaflet depicting Boris and his manager.

'This—' He stabbed his finger at the manager's portrait. 'This is the dead body I saw in the lake.'

They were all gratifyingly stunned.

'Are you sure?'

'No doubt about it. That was the body I saw! It says here he's Boris's manager, but he's not, is he? Boris's manager is another geezer.'

Christian took the leaflet and studied it closely.

'No. You're right. But that couple who are minding Boris say they are called Turkin. I know that. I heard Mr Harlech introduce them to one of the teachers. Mr and Mrs Igor Turkin.'

'Let's ask Boris,' Jodie said.

'Show him the leaflet,' Nutty said. 'They've murdered the real Igor Turkin and are pretending to be him.'

'What's the motive?'

'Boris,' John Pike said. 'Making money out of Boris. He's worth a fortune, or will be at the rate he's going on, and they get ten per cent, or whatever agents get.'

Boris had his head in the wardrobe, choosing his clothes for the concert.

'Ask him,' said Hoomey.

'How?'

'Show him the leaflet.'

'Steady on,' said Christian. 'If this is true – and we don't know it is – we don't want them to know we've sussed it, do we? Arnold's having a rough enough time as it is. I think we ought to sit on it until we can get a bit more proof.'

'Like what?' asked Nutty. 'Arnold's corpse?'

'No. We've got to keep Arnold right with us; it's the only way he's safe.'

'Fort Knox has relaxed. We'll take him with us this afternoon and keep him under our noses all the time.'

'Yes, in with the crowd.'

'But does Boris know what's going on?'

The question was in all their minds. Yet Boris seemed to have a benign and innocent presence. It was hard to believe that he knew a murder had been committed. He knew they were hiding Arnold, but it occurred to them all that he didn't know who from.

When they went down to lunch, leaving Arnold in the wardrobe, Mrs Knox met them at the bottom of the stairs and actually congratulated them on their handling of Boris.

'He seems so much happier now he's with you. Those managers of his are a very serious bunch – they do no good, pressurizing him. We've all noticed how much more relaxed he is. Well done, boys.'

Meanwhile Arnold locked himself in the bedroom and changed into some dry clothes. He lay down on the best bed and pulled the eiderdown over him and dozed off. He dreamed he was in the hall with the white skulls looking down on him from all sides. The dead deer were saying, 'Watch out, watch out,' and in his dream he heard the sound of the door handle being turned. He woke up in a sweat, opened his eyes and saw the bedroom door handle gently turning. The bed was only a couple of metres from the door. He stared at it, pop-eyed, and heard soft breathing, and the slight scuffle of a body pressing against the firmness of the lock. He held his breath. Of course! His antagonist only had to remove him while everyone was downstairs – down the fire-escape . . . a skirmish behind the outhouses and his body could be dumped in the heather as no doubt it was meant to have been dumped the night before!

Arnold knew he had never lived as dangerously as this. He had only turned the key in the lock as an afterthought. He lay in a cold sweat, eyes fixed on the old-fashioned porcelain doorknob. It was tried twice more, turning slowly until it came to the resistance of the lock, a long silence, then the creaking of a floorboard told of retreat. Another door closed along the corridor . . . the door to the fire-escape? Was it really Boris's minder who was after him, or someone else he had no knowledge of? He lay with his heart thumping like a piston, pure funk and self-pity overwhelming him.

When the others came back with a selection of lunch (a large dollop of shepherd's pie and steamed treacle pudding in the bottom of a violin case) they found him shaking and tearful.

'It's really serious – we ought to tell somebody,' Jodie suggested. 'It's not a joke any more.'

'What do you think, Arnold?' Christian asked.

'I'd rather stay with you.'

'It's a terrible risk.'

'Not this afternoon, is it? In the orchestra? We could think about it tonight, later . . . '

Arnold didn't want to be handed back to Authority. No-one would show him much sympathy. He had told too many tales in the past. The others, honest and God-fearing as they were, had no knowledge of how the police treated such as he, who scattered lies to hide his passage as guests scattered confetti at a wedding. His past was catching up with him.

'Well, it's true – there's no time now. We've got to be on the coach in a quarter of an hour. We've scraped together a bit of uniform for you – shirt and tie and these trousers – bit large probably but they'll have to do. Get changed and eat your dinner and you can carry the violin case out to the coach. We'll keep right with you.'

Already, with the gang round him, Arnold felt better. His confidence flooded back. But the others were now slightly itchy, feeling their responsibilities closing in: the joke had gone farther than they had intended. However more immediate worries were looming: the first concert was an occasion for nerves and – horrors—!

'She's counting everyone on the bus!' Hoomey reported back.

Arnold was already stowing his empty violin case in the luggage compartment. The two coaches were parked side by side. Christian grabbed Arnold and propelled him towards the second coach where another teacher was counting them on board – anything to avoid Fort Knox.

Nutty summed up the situation. 'There'll be too many and there'll be a recount and Arn'll get discovered. Here, I'll stay behind. The coaches'll go and I'll get a lift with one of the cars – say I forgot something – went back for it and missed the bus.'

'Suppose you can't get a lift! You mustn't go missing! There's lots of cymbal-crashing this afternoon.'

'Don't be daft, of course I'll get a lift! Get Arnold to unload my stuff.'

It was the best move in the circumstances. Arnold was counted by the teacher who wasn't looking for a boy with hair like a lavatory brush – she then went across and added her numbers to Mrs Knox's and as the tally was correct the two buses departed. Nutty was left in the courtyard, eyeing up the possibilities.

Not all the adults were going. Mrs Knox said she was going to spend the afternoon with her paperwork and went back to the house. Mr Harlech was going but had an enquiring and bossy nature which made Nutty feel it would be best to avoid him, and quite a few of the parents were squashing five to a car which was no go. She decided to ask one of the teachers, a lady harpist, who was travelling to the concert with her harp. She was going to give a recital in the evening in the same hall.

She was a stringy, twittery lady called Mildred Manners with a rather ancient estate car. The harp filled all the back and overlapped rather into the front seat, where Nutty invited herself.

'Of course, my dear, I'll be glad of the company. And you can help me with my harp. You look a strong girl.'

Oh great, thought Nutty. She was a strong girl, and revelled in it, but sometimes she wished she was a willowy wand like Jodie. Not that Jodie was willowy by nature. Nutty, used to being the boss, sometimes found that she was doing what Jodie decided. She liked her friends in the orchestra, the best reason for staying: no-one could accuse her of being musical. Christian and Jodie really worked at it, and John Pike was brilliant. Where he practised Nutty had no idea, making that sort of noise. When she let off her cymbals at home the lady next door hammered on the wall with her poker.

'Must be difficult, being a harpist. Moving it around, I mean,' she ventured.

'Yes. Like the double bass. We should have been flautists. What are you, dear?'

'Only cymbals.'

'Oh, what fun. It must be satisfying to make a really loud noise.'

'Yes, it's lovely.'

She wasn't a bad old stick. Poor harpists could do no more than ripple along, however hard they pinged and plucked. A harp was a grand piano standing up, pulled instead of pushed and with nothing like the power. At least Boris didn't have his piano in his luggage. Nutty wondered if Miss Manners knew anything about Boris's manager. She was on the committee and must be in the know. She decided to fish.

'The Russian boy is ace, isn't he?'

'Extraordinarily talented. Aren't we lucky to have him? He was being acclaimed in Moscow, and Mr Harlech happened to be over there when he won the big prize. Mr Harlech found he was staying in the same hotel as Boris's manager so he got friendly with him, offered him hospitality over here if he would like to come. He's very quick-thinking, Mr Harlech.'

'Is that Mr Turkin, Boris's manager?'

Miss Manners frowned.

'Well, there was a bit of a mix-up. The Mr Turkin with Boris now isn't the manager Mr Harlech met. The one Mr Harlech met in Russia came over with Boris and Mr Harlech met him, and they had a group of friends with them. But apparently the manager was taken ill, and went off to some hospital in London – this was just before we were to start the tour – and fortunately the friend said he would step in and take his place. So we decided to call him Mr Turkin instead – his own name is quite unpronounceable. And of course the name Turkin is on the publicity as Boris's manager so it was easier not to change it.'

'I thought Mr Turkin wasn't the same man as in the photographs,' Nutty remarked. Her voice was unconcerned – 'I should be an actress!' she thought, for she could feel her pulse hammering with excitement. They had really cracked it! The present Mr Turkin had done for Boris's manager, chucked him in the lake and taken his job. No doubt when they got back and Mr Harlech wanted to renew acquaintance it would be discovered that the poor ill Russian had flown home for further treatment. The Russians would think he was still in England. He could disappear without any trouble at all.

Nutty stared out of the window to cool her excitement. As soon as they got back tonight they would have to go to Mr Harlech and tell him the story. Take the pressure off poor Arnold, the only one who could give evidence.

Mildred had taken a short cut. 'I'm sure this little road is quicker – I took it when I was on holiday – nicer too. I hate motorways, don't you?'

It wound steeply uphill, hairpinning between banks of heather and stands of pine. Rain flicked across the windscreen. Nutty started to bite her fingernails with excitement, impatient to get back to the others and tell them of her discovery. Mildred clashed her gears into a more amiable whine and her old car ground on over the potholes.

CHAPTER SEVEN

The orchestra was tuning up. The big hall was full and the best rows all filled with the educational big-wigs and music buffs of the Scottish Highlands. Arnold, feeling somewhat constrained in his borrowed orchestra uniform, discovered he was a part of 'the cultural heritage of music-making countries from all over Europe'. There was a fair amount of speechifying first and, the drive having been much longer than they had expected, it was early evening when the concert started.

Much to Arnold's concern, Nutty hadn't yet appeared.

'It doesn't matter,' John Pike said. 'She's got nothing to do for forty-five minutes. She's bound to be here by then. Keep your nut down, for heaven's sake.'

Arnold shrunk between the cliffs of John Pike's timpani. He was glad Pike could be so confident.

Hoomey was fussing because Nutty wasn't there to prompt him.

'What if she doesn't come?'

'Arnie'll do it,' John Pike said.

Arnold felt his stomach zooming up and down with fright. The thought was almost as bad as watching door handles turning. He glanced at Pike and saw he was grinning. He couldn't argue because this is where he had longed to be, in the bosom of the orchestra, and as the music started crashing out all round him he felt comforted, cocooned by the noise. It was a wall all round him, cutting off danger. The magnificent Jodie was sawing away below him, yellow hair tossing, and round the bend the noble Christian was throwing a tune back at the violins, repeating their theme like a mating bird, over and over. The decibels of John Pike's drums moved up to danger level in his right ear. What a racket! Arnold found it hard to credit the amazing company he had homed into.

When the piece finished the hall burst into an even louder din of appreciation, clapping and stamping. All the players turned up different music. Arnold turned agitated eyes up to John Pike.

'No cymbals in this. Relax.'

Arnold relaxed.

John Pike bent down towards him in the

gathering hush. 'But if she doesn't turn up for the next one, mate, you'll be in business.'

'Funny,' said Mildred Manners, as the car went bouncing over large potholes and Nutty was obliged to turn round to try and fend off the harp that threatened to brain her, 'I thought this lane went down to the main road. It seems to be petering out.'

Truly observed . . . the lane turned into dirt and finished at a padlocked gate in a stone wall.

'Oh dear.'

Mildred went into reverse, turning, and the back wheels sank into a bog. She went into first and revved up and the wheels flew round spewing out black muck in all directions.

'I think you'll have to push, dear. I'll try again.'

'It's in too deep,' Nutty said, having a look.

'Oh, I'm sure not! Just give it a try!'

The car was much too heavy, Nutty could see, for even her beef to make any difference, but she did as she was told, put her body to the rear of the car and got drenched in black squidge for her pains.

'Oh dear.'

Mildred got out to look.

'We'll have to put something under the wheels, won't we?'

The harp, Nutty thought crossly.

She glanced at her watch. 'Cripes!'

Gloom turned to panic. 'The concert starts in forty minutes!'

'Oh dear. Silly me!'

There was no farm or habitation within sight, only the everlasting hill covered with bracken and heather.

'We'll have to pull up stuff and put it under the wheels,' Nutty decided. 'Cover up the mud.'

'Oh, but my hands!' complained Mildred.

Nutty started pulling. The cymbals didn't need a lot of finesse after all.

John Pike leant down to Arnold during the applause and said, 'You'd better get up and look as if you're the cymbalist. Your crashes don't come till near the end so she could still make it. If not, you'll just have to do your best.'

'I can't!' Arnold squeaked.

'You've bloomin' got to! Hoomey's hopeless, he's tried before. We can't have him panicking. He knows where the crashes come though, so he can give you the prod. D'you hear, Hoomey?'

'Yes!'

'You both owe it to Nutty not to make a hash of it.' John Pike looked very severe, a real public school prefect. His voice was stern, dropping as the applause started to die away.

'Can't you do it?' Arnold whispered.

'I'm going full bore as it is – no way. Get up now, stand behind them. If you do it right, no-one will notice anything amiss. That's what matters.'

Arnold got up and stood in the back row, feeling as large as an elephant. He was trembling like an aspen leaf. Hoomey stood beside him, white-faced.

'Where's she got to? Perhaps Claws has got her?'

'Don't be daft!'

Arnold eyed the cymbals that stood before him on their stand – two large discs of brass with handles to grasp them by. He remembered Nutty holding them aloft, arms stretched out, a manic glint in her eye, tongue between her teeth, waiting for the moment of impact. If she could do it . . . she was only a girl . . .

All the brass instruments went into action at a nod from Mr Carruthers and Arnold froze as John Pike started an unholy racket beside him, a drum roll to end all drum rolls. Arnold felt his blood curdling. It was familiar, this piece. Oh, please, he prayed, let it be all right!

Part of the orchestra now, Arnold felt the music moving through his guts. He was all stirred up, waiting. It was a piece called *Finlandia* by Sibelius – it had wonderful tunes that you had to wait for. It had just sounded one long mess the first time he had heard it but now it had got a hold of him like a hit in the charts. John Pike had to work really hard building up the crescendos and then gonging his biggest drum with enormous drumsticks like boxing gloves on sticks, giving almighty swipes, his red hair flopping across a sweaty forehead, blue eyes glittering, until all the strings came sweeping in with the marvellous tune. Then when they died away Christian took it up alone, slow and heart-rending, and Mr Carruthers closed his eyes and put on a really fatuous face as if he was getting a call from God. Then it was all go again, and Arnold picked up his cymbals, no longer scared but dying to give them a bash.

'Not yet!' Hoomey squeaked.

John Pike was going full blast – no wonder he was such a stocky, muscled fellow, good as a game of soccer this, Arnold thought, and Hoomey gave him a nudge and said, 'Coming up any minute!' and Arnold lifted the heavy brass cymbals and brought them together with a wonderful crash, louder even than John Pike's. The brass was competing too, deafening the back row.

'And again,' said Hoomey.

WHAM! Hey, this was terrific! Every time John Pike finished a drum roll Arnold crowned it with a WHAM!

Hoomey was pulling at his arm.

'Shut up!' he hissed. 'You're finished!'

But Arnold got in two more before the finish. It would have been three if Hoomey hadn't physically restrained him.

The audience went mad, clapping and cheering and stamping, and all the various parts of the orchestra got up separately for a bow. Arnold, seeing John Pike bow, bowed too. He did not notice Mr Carruthers giving him a hard look.

It was the interval now, before Boris played his piano concerto. John Pike took Arnold's arm and said, 'Cripes, you went potty! Everyone's noticed you now, you idiot! We'd all better keep our heads down now, else they'll be after us.'

There were refreshments in the interval but Arnold was guided outside by his elders and betters and dumped on the school lawn. Jodie and Christian found them.

'You're an absolute nutter!' Jodie hissed. 'You'd think you wanted everyone to see you up there, crashing away!'

'Fantastic!' Christian was grinning. 'A natural! Your timing was splendid. If Sibelius had put all those crashes in the score – which he didn't, being a restrained sort of bloke – that's where he'd have had 'em, all the same, right where you decided.'

Arnold wasn't sure whether he was in the doghouse or whether he had just discovered the meaning of life. He was on a high, skating along the tops of Sibelius's thunder. Those cymbals were really something! His hands really hurt.

'It was brill! I'd like to do it again!'

'Actually, you were pretty good.' John Pike was smiling too.

'Is there any more? In the next . . . if Nutty doesn't turn up?'

'There's a piece we finish with . . . nothing in Boris's concerto. I wonder where Nutty's got to?'

She still didn't arrive. They filched some refreshments (Arnold only got two ginger biscuits), then they were bundling back on stage again. This time they insisted he got under the drum covers at the back, completely out of sight. Mr Carruthers was sending dagger glances up towards the timpani. Boris swept on in his best suit, rather tight and of a dubious dark blue, and bowed extravagantly to the welcoming cheers. John Pike picked up his drumsticks and, when everything had gone quiet, started this tremendous roll. Arnold could feel it coming up through his seatbones and vibrating right through his rib-cage. The excitement of it was tremendous. It made his hair stand on end. And then Boris came crashing in to join him. Ba ba BOM! Ba ba BOM! Ba ba BOM! Arnold wriggled with excitement. It was sweating hot under the plastic cover. He thought perhaps he had a fever the way he felt. He itched to be cymbaling again. The music broke out all round him, sweeping and sliding and banging and crashing. He realized he had a hell of a headache.

At the end when Boris was bowing to left, right and centre and the audience was cheering and stamping again, Nutty arrived amongst the timpani. She was covered with mud and had some sprigs of heather stuck in her hair. She slapped down the hopeful Arnold with a brisk request to get out of her way.

'Aren't you supposed to be *hiding*?'

She dropped the drum cover back over him like putting a parrot to bed.

Hoomey said indignantly, 'He did your cymbals in *Finlandia*. He was really good!'

John Pike grinned. 'He was ace. You'll lose your job if you don't look out.'

'Yeah, well, old Claws must have taken note. He's here, you know! And I've found out—'

Mr Carruthers tapped his baton imperiously on his music stand. John Pike just had time to hiss, 'But we're going to tell all when we get back, aren't we? We've only got to guard him for another hour or two!'

Arnold, crouching in his plastic cave, flinched as the music broke out all round him. He was all stirred up, but whether by his recent experiences or the thought of being exposed shortly to the mercies of Mrs Knox, Mr Harlech and all he could not tell. It was agony trying to sit still, the blood hammering through his veins so that he felt breathless. He thought he was going off his nut. What on earth was going to happen when they revealed that Boris's keepers were dyed-in-the-wool crooks? Arnold thought it would go down like a lead balloon. It would ruin the tour. Everything was getting rather out of control.

As he sat there, cocooned in swooshing, stirring noise, he wished with all his heart that he could stay, for ever, within the battlements of the school orchestra. Stupid as he was, he trusted implicitly the decisions of the General's son Christian, the stolid John Pike, even the stout-hearted girls – girls being a definite turn-off in his life so far. (His mother called herself a girl.) Even Hoomey, a real wimp, was transparently well-meaning. He saw that the really noble thing would be to get up and go away, far away, where Claws would never find him again and nor would Christian and the gang. He ought to back out now, over the edge of the staging and out through the back door, go to the station and catch the train to London. Leave them all in the clear.

He couldn't. He had no money. Nor the will. He wasn't noble, after all. He wanted them to see him through, even if it brought them all down. He tried to make excuses for himself, but he knew he was a pretty hopeless case. He was good at cymbals though! The little thought kept surfacing, with a rush of good cheer.

The music finished and the applause took over. It seemed to go on for ages. This, Arnold thought, was the beginning of the end. He crouched himself up, heart beating audibly, hating everything. The staging shook as everyone started to push back their chairs and prepare to leave. There was a great hubbub of conversation and general noise. John Pike whipped the cover off him.

'Keep your nut down. We've got to decide what to do next.'

'There's tea in the school. Over the road. That's what's next,' Hoomey said hopefully.

'Idiot, about Arnie!'

Christian and Jodie came over, shutting their instruments away in their cases. They looked serious. The stage was rapidly clearing.

'Listen,' said Nutty. 'What I found out. Old Mildred told me—' She recounted Miss Manners' story of Boris's keepers. The others were very impressed.

'It all makes sense.'

'We can't go on hiding it up. When we get back—' But Christian looked anguished at the thought. Arnold knew he was wishing they had never got involved.

'Come on,' he said firmly, in his General's voice. 'We'll carry on as usual. Keep Arn in the middle. Carruthers might come to find out about the new cymbalist. We want to keep out of his way. There's just a chance, after all, that – that – well, we might . . . '

'It's not fair to hide it up, not to Arnold, or Boris, or anybody,' John Pike said stoutly. 'Even if it does mess up the music fortnight.'

Christian looked agonized again. 'No,' he agreed.

'Do you think Boris knows what's going on?' Jodie said.

'I keep asking myself . . . I think not,' Christian said.

'No! He can't know.' Nutty was positive. 'Not about his friends trying to knock out Arn.'

'No, not that. He might know about the first Mr Turkin being removed though.'

'Not if they could avoid it, surely?' Jodie said. 'I bet they just told him he was ill, gone home. That would account for his being a bit nervous, not very sure of them. I mean, the first Mr Turkin must have been his friend.'

Everyone was trailing out of the big hall into the street. Across the road was a school where tea was being laid on in the hall. The coaches were parked outside the hall and the school precincts were full of parked cars, including the mud-sprayed, heather-tagged estate car of Mildred Manners with the harp still in the back. A great crowd was milling about, both audience and orchestra, and there seemed no immediate danger. Murder could hardly be committed in such a situation.

'What'll we do then?' Nutty demanded.

'Tea for now,' said Christian.

They stowed their instruments back in the coach and crossed the road to the school, keeping an eye open for the people they wanted to avoid. The school hall was buzzing. They scrummed for sandwiches and cups of tea, elbows well out, and backed out into the schoolyard to eat. The ever-present mountains seemed to lean over the street, sharply etched in an evening glow of forgiving sunlight. For a moment it was warm. They lined up against the stone wall dividing the school grounds from the road, hitching their bottoms on the uncomfortable rocks.

'If Arn stays around you'll lose your job,' John Pike grinned at Nutty. 'He's a natural.'

Nutty glared from over her tea mug. 'I was doing him a favour! Look where it got me! Don't push your luck, Arn boy.'

'When you tell 'em, tonight, they'll send me back to London,' Arnold said sadly. 'It'll all fall apart.'

'Oh, come on,' said Christian. 'You'll be a star witness. It's not like being the one they're after.'

'They won't forget they're after me. Not afterwards.'

'Well, s'like being a grass,' Hoomey said eagerly. 'You'll get off for helping the police.'

'Hmm.' Arnold wasn't so sure.

'Hey, here's Boris.'

Boris was approaching, smiling, with a large piece of chocolate cake on a plate.

He held it up and articulated carefully, 'Delicious. Good Lord!'

'Hey, well done, Boris boy! Speak Engleeshski!' Nutty grinned.

'Hi,' said Boris. 'Lampshade!' He smiled at Nutty.

The others all rocked about.

'Go on, tell him you love him, Nutty. You looked it up!'

'Oh, shut up!' Nutty had gone bright red. 'And lampshade to you too, Boris,' she added.

'Good Lord!' said Boris.

His vocabulary extended no further, and there was no way of asking him if he knew his keepers were murderers. He took a large bite of chocolate cake and a blob of chocolate cream fell down his cream silk tie.

'Good Lord!' he said.

'Lampshade!' said Nutty.

Arnold wished he'd seen the chocolate cake.

'I'm going to get a piece,' he said.

'Not on your own,' Christian said. 'Hoomey, you go with him.'

The two of them disappeared back into the hall. A few minutes later Mildred Manners fluttered her way across to Nutty and said, 'Could you help me with my harp, dear? Just to unload it?'

The boys offered to help. They all wandered over to her car and she opened up the back.

Christian and John Pike nobly went to lift out the harp while Boris stood around not knowing what to do with his chocolate cake. Just as the two boys were edging the instrument carefully through the back aperture Hoomey came tearing round the side of the building shouting at the top of his voice.

'He's gone! He's gone!'

Christian straightened up. 'Hoomey!' he bellowed.

Hoomey changed course like a hunted hare and sprang towards them.

'He's got him – that man – Ferretface! Quick! There! Look!'

He was pointing out into the road. The Russian's Citroen was just in the act of backing out of the side street where it was parked, driven by Ferretface, with Arnold sagging in the front seat.

'He hit him!' Hoomey wailed.

Christian and John Pike dropped the harp as one man. As it twanged on to the tarmac Christian took a flying leap into the driving seat.

'Get in!' he shouted.

They leapt into the back. John Pike slammed the tailgate down and jumped into the front seat as Christian started the engine. The old car shot backwards out of the schoolyard. Ahead of it, the Citroen sped away down the street.

Hoomey squeaked, 'He went to the loo – there wasn't anyone there, and that man – him! – he followed him in – I saw him – he dragged him out and hit him—'

'Did he see you?' Christian snapped.

'No. I was at the top of the corridor, waiting for him. I came for you!'

'Why didn't you sock him one?' Nutty shouted at him. 'You're hopeless, Hoomey! You could've stopped him!'

'You're sure he didn't see you? He thinks he's got Arnold away without anyone seeing?'

'Yes!'

Nutty, looking behind, saw Miss Manners crouching, pop-eyed, over her harp, and Boris standing looking after them with a puzzled look on his face (no doubt saying, 'Good Lord!'). Behind him, Mr and Mrs Turkin were hurrying to collect him up.

'What are we going to do?' she asked Christian, fearing the worst.

'Arn's only chance is for us to follow him,' Christian said tersely. 'That geezer's going to take him somewhere remote and do him in. We've got to stop him!'

'The rest of the gang know what's going on,' Nutty said grimly. 'They've collected Boris already.'

'Probably come after us,' John Pike said.

'What are we going to do?' Hoomey wailed.

'Rescue Arnold, of course!' Nutty shrieked. 'Because you're such a dimwit, Hoomey, letting it happen! You were supposed to be guarding him!'

As they skidded round the bend out of the village they all saw the black Citroen ahead of them, accelerating up a road that led over the forested hillside. Christian straightened up and put his foot down. With five of them in it, Miss Manners' old Ford shuddered manfully in pursuit.

'Are you sure we're doing the right thing?' Jodie asked doubtfully, looking back.

'No,' said Christian. 'I'm sure we're not, but it's too late now.'

'If we lose them, Arnie's lost!' said John Pike.

Christian changed down as the hill met them. It was up to him now, and Mildred's old banger.

Poor Arnie!

CHAPTER EIGHT

The road they were following led to a tourist camping site on a hillside overlooking a lake. Ferretface drove past and took another unsurfaced route marked 'Unsuitable for Motors'. It was by now seven o'clock, a grey evening promising drizzle, and there were no campers to be seen. Only early lights shining in the big tents showed any sign of life, and Christian did not stop to plead help.

'Mustn't lose him or Arn'll be a goner!'

Afterwards, they supposed one of them could have tumbled out and raised an alarm, but by the time they thought of this they were well past and jerking up the mountainside desperately trying to keep within sight of the Citroen's occasional bright brake-lights. Christian had grated into second gear and Mildred's old car was labouring.

They were all in a state of high anxiety and excitement. Christian, totally occupied with his driving, said nothing and John Pike at his side was quiet and grim, trying to work out whether things were quite as serious as he rather thought they were. In the back Hoomey was white-faced, trying not to burst into tears – it was all *his* fault, after all, that had been made quite clear to him – while the two girls bounced about urging Christian on.

'Five of us – we'll get 'im!' Nutty was crowing. 'C'm on, Chris, put your foot down!'

'He can't *really* be wanting to murder him, surely?' Jodie appealed. 'It can't be that important?'

'Arnie is a real threat to their success – you think about it,' John Pike pointed out. 'No-one suspects what they've done. Only Arnie. Arnie knows more than is good for him.'

'But so do we, now,' Jodie said.

'Yeah, that's what I'm worried about!'

'You don't think—!' Nutty stopped bouncing and leaned over the seat, breathing down Christian's neck. 'He'll murder all of us?'

Hoomey started to cry. He stared out of the window, trying to convince himself he was on holiday, having a great time.

'He can't,' Jodie said bluntly. 'There's too many of us!'

The road hairpinned upwards. Christian crashed gears valiantly but managed to keep the old car from stalling. The gravelly surface spun out from beneath the spinning wheels and there was a strong smell of burning rubber. But the gradient eased gradually and the road came out on to a high plateau. On the left beyond a flattish stretch the land dipped into a deep gorge with a stream in spate running down towards a far valley; the hillside reared up steeply beyond, with a crown of rocks standing black against the rain-steely sky. Ahead there was sparse forest with high mountains beyond, and mountains rimmed the view to the right. There appeared to be nowhere to go ahead, but the road slashed on across a sea of heather and the tail-lights of the Citroen were still in sight, fireflies in the gathering gloom.

'Does he know we're following him?' John Pike wondered.

'If he does, I wouldn't have thought he'd have his lights on,' Christian said. 'That's why I'm not using them.'

'He's slowing down,' Nutty said.

Christian lifted his foot a fraction off the floor.

'He's going left! There can't be a road down there?'

The ground fell away in that direction, but there was no doubt the rear-lights were bouncing downhill. Shortly they disappeared. Christian accelerated again.

The detour was solved when they came to a fork in the road. A cart-track fell away to the left where the Citroen had gone. A footpath direction sign pointed the way.

'Antrim Falls,' they read.

Christian accelerated onward, not taking the side road.

'What are you doing?' Nutty squeaked.

'We stand more chance if we can surprise him! It can't be far down there – Pike and I'll run down. If we take the car he'll hear us as soon as he stops his own engine.'

'We'll come!' the girls cried with one breath.

'No! If we want help we'll yell. Otherwise stay here!'

His voice was sharply General-ish. The girls subsided, scowling, and the two boys sprinted away downhill, leaping across the heather. They were dressed in their orchestra gear, black trousers, black jerseys, white shirts and pale grey ties, and in the murk faded quickly. They seemed to move exceedingly fast.

Jodie and Nutty sat, deflated, realizing how scared they were. This was a bleak place to be in with a murderer and doing nothing was harder than speeding to the rescue.

'Suppose—?' Jodie started, and hesitated.

Hoomey was shivering. The landscape was grey in every direction, save for a lemon-yellow streak of fading sunlight over the far mountains. It was still and windless; the rain was like a drifting mist, and the booming of the stream as it hurtled down its narrow gorge was loud on the evening air.

'It can't be far away – hark at it,' Jodie said.

'Perhaps he's going to throw him in,' Nutty said. 'Good way to get rid of anyone.'

They opened the windows and sat waiting, listening. A cool breeze riffled the heather and a hare ran away ahead of them down the track. Nutty found her initial excitement draining slowly away and a nasty feeling, much like fear, taking over. The scene was not cosy in any way at all, the grey premature dusk stealing up from the valleys with faint lines of mist lying in the crooks and declivities all round them. The booming of the water through the nearby gorge was suggestive and chilling. The heat of the moment had worn off and it was clear that there was only one reason why the Russian murderer had taken that downward path towards the Falls. Nutty found herself shivering, but the awareness of Jodie's tense, hard face watching the valley without a show of any emotion tightened her resolve. The boys might need them and, if they did, need them pretty badly.

Christian and John Pike were fit with their tough school sports experience and negotiated the rough ground only marginally slower than the Citroen ahead of them. The rear-lights shone strongly as the car lurched and braked down the uneven road. The boys had to slow down, doubled closely into the heather.

They both knew they needed a plan.

'Attack him first?'

'He's very powerful ... get as close as we can ...'

'He must be going to chuck him over the bridge—'

'Cripes! If he does—'

The ground fell sharply away, suddenly, and on the other side of the stream the hillside crowded close, boulder strewn, making a sudden deep gorge into which the water fell with a hollow booming noise. With trees clinging to the steep sides and an ancient arched bridge over the lip of the waterfall, the murder venue chosen by Ferretface was a tourist beauty spot, complete with car park, litter bin and National Trust collecting-box. The spray from the Falls made a mist against the black hillside and the dampness was like a cold shroud settling over their faces as they watched the black car. It went past the car park and came to a halt on the threshold of the bridge.

Christian and John Pike scrambled down the bank of heather, the noise of the waterfall covering the sound of their approach. Fast as they ran, they were still out of reach as Ferretface ran round to the passenger seat and dragged Arnold bodily out on to the road. Arnold seemed to have no fight and made no resistance, very small and limp in the grasp of his adversary, dragged without a struggle to the parapet of the bridge.

Christian and John Pike screamed with one voice and leapt violently off the steep heather bank. The Russian turned and they saw his astonished face, white and gleaming below them. But immediately, convulsively, he scooped up Arnie's legs, shoved them over the parapet and with one quick shove sent him toppling over the top.

'No!'

The shock horror of his action galvanized the two boys. They veered off and plunged down the side of the gorge at a pace which in cold blood was suicidal. The waterfall fell unimpeded into a deep pool below them and then overflowed over a wide lip into lower pools and wild, foaming reaches which they could hear, if not see, in the spray-shot gloom. Falling rather than climbing down the cliff, they grabbed branches and tufts of ferns as best they could to steady progress, sending down showers of loose rock. Once Arnie's body went over the lip and down into the rocky reaches below it would be pounded to death, such was the spate of water after the incessant rain –

they both knew that. But the drop into the deep pool was not a killer. Save—

'He can't swim!' John Pike jerked out. 'He told me!'

Christian made a grab for a birch branch which broke off in his hand and fell the last three metres into the deep pool. The water was ice-cold and he came up feeling that he had had his chest smashed in. The falling stream above roared in his ears so that he had to shout to John Pike, dithering on a ledge above him.

'Where – where—?' But he had no breath in his body.

John Pike pointed. Christian tossed his hair out of his eyes and looked across the foaming pool, feeling awesome currents tugging at his legs, already taking him off willy-nilly away from the bank. He was a strong swimmer and not frightened, only frightened of not getting Arnie before he went over the top. Or sank. He panicked momentarily, not seeing anything else in the pool.

'Over there!'

John Pike was pointing all the time, hopping about on his ledge like an agitated monkey.

Christian swam in the direction indicated, across the pool, and felt himself plucked and buffeted so that he came up against the sill without meaning to. The rocks seemed to crash into him, and the pull threatened to take him over the top. It was very strong and terrifyingly persistent, like a giant hand shoving. He swam against it, facing the waterfall, fending off with his feet, far more frightened than he wanted to be. If he had to come back with Arnie it would be touch and go to make it. Yet he knew there was no getting out on the far side: the rock was sheer, even over-hanging, and there were no ledges at water-level to offer sanctuary.

He could see Arnie now, bobbing like discarded litter on the far side, slowly approaching the sill. He was holding his face above water and dog-paddling, but merely keeping afloat. As he came out from the rocks he started to be swept more and more rapidly towards the sill.

There was no time to lose. Christian kicked himself off and swam towards him with his powerful crawl, resisting the current by the sheer strength of his stroke. He closed gradually with Arnie who, seeing deliverance, started to panic. His face went under, bobbed up once, and went under again.

Christian threshed down, catching him by his loose jersey. He turned on to his back and kicked with all his strength to get back under the relative tranquillity of the far wall of rock, heaving Arnie with him, cupped under the chin. Pure funk made a splendid impetus. The roaring of the water made it seem that there was no world outside this treacherous pool; it was like being thrown into a deep pit and pressed down and in and kept there.

And 'kept there' was the relevant phrase, he realized, as he homed suddenly into a perfectly still and currentless back eddy under the wall of the far rock. Kicking so hard, he found there was suddenly no resistance, and he came up quite violently against the rock wall, nearly knocking himself out. The relief was tremendous. He relaxed, and heaved Arnold into a more comfortable grasp. Arnold was squeaking incoherently like a drowned hamster, but mercifully not wriggling overmuch.

John Pike was still on his ledge, but Christian could hear nothing he was shouting for the sound of the water. He indicated as much, and John Pike then went into a great mime, sweeping his arms round in circles, and Christian gathered that he was suggesting it might be better to come back to the bank beneath him by swimming behind the waterfall, rather than across the sill. Christian thought it was worth a try. There was a big scooped cave of rock behind the foaming cauldron where the water hit bottom, and it looked positively calm and peaceful. Whether it was, remained to be seen.

'Just relax, Arnie. I'll take you. But don't flail about, for goodness sake. I won't let go.'

Arnie's wet hair stood straight up as if an electric current was running through it. He seemed to have taken in the situation, but was, quite understandably, jibbering with fright and quite unable to make conversation. Christian took him in a firm grip and kicked off hard, heading for inside the waterfall. To his great relief the water was comparatively undisturbed. Several backwashes buffeted them about but there was no gripping current tearing them to where they didn't want to go, only the impressive sight of ten metres of water plummeting down from heaven with a roar like thunder to land far too close to their eardrums. Somehow Christian managed to remember that a steamer made a trippers' journey round the back of the Niagara Falls – had John Pike remembered this nugget of information? He kicked on, the icy cold beginning to get to him, cramping his lungs. Swimming with Arnold in tow was no joke.

John Pike had managed to decamp to water level and was holding out the substantial branch which had broken off in Christian's hand. It made a sort of harbour wall and Christian was relieved to stop swimming and take it in his grasp. John Pike heaved him in and leaned down to swap his hand for the branch.

'Take Arnie!' Christian muttered. For a little lad he was a ton weight to tow.

There was only a tiny bit of bank, a ledge of rock from which John Pike leaned down to extend one hand, the other held fast to a useful and well-rooted alder sapling. Arnold reached out and was hauled ashore like a bundle of wet washing, then Christian, and the three of them started to climb up the bank before they froze to death. There was no breath for talking. Arnold was in a state of trance and needed much pulling and shoving. He was shaking and ghost-white and could not speak.

'Shock,' said Christian. 'And he's had a bang on the head – he might be concussed.'

'Cripes, d'you think that rat is still up there, waiting for us?' Pike stopped suddenly.

They were halfway up the cliff-face – both good climbers, it seemed easier going up than coming down – and the gorge was dark and the rain now lashing down. Christian stopped, surprised he hadn't thought of the possibility himself. Then he shrugged.

'Hope for the best!'

But the car had gone. When they dragged Arnold over the last slab of rock they found the tourist beauty spot deserted. Coming down the track towards them was Mildred's old Cortina with Jodie at the wheel.

'He drove back down the valley, the way we came up! As soon as we saw him go we came down.'

'Thank heaven for that! Here, help get Arnie in the car – he's just about all out.'

They explained what had happened and the girls hauled out the blankets Mildred used for cocooning her harp in and handed them to the dripping boys.

'Put the heater on!' They all crowded back into the car, and Jodie reversed it into the car park and out again, heading back up the hill. The rain slammed down and the sky ahead was black. They were all talking at once, astounded by their adventure.

'He's a *murderer*!'

'Suppose you'd been too late! Poor old Arnie! Are you OK, Arnie?'

Arnold still felt close to death, but knew he wasn't any more, which helped his brain if not his body. The warmth of his orchestral friends was reviving him.

'Lucky you were in time to fish him out!'

'Cor, suppose—?'

'Shut *up*, Hoomey!'

The car's wheels spun and Jodie had no lower gear to change into.

'Who's volunteering to push?'

Christian said, 'It's almost out of petrol.'

'I was pretending not to notice,' Jodie said.

John Pike and Nutty got out to push and they managed to get going again.

'I don't think we should drive down in these conditions,' Christian said. 'It's asking for trouble. Besides which, the petrol gauge is on zero.'

'And the tyres are all bald,' John Pike said.

'There was a stone house up the valley,' Nutty said. 'We noticed it while we were waiting. One of those old hunting lodges, or a bothy or something. Empty, but it had a roof and windows and things. We could wait there till it gets light again.'

'They might come looking for us – a helicopter! Fort Knox, I mean, not the Russians. If we don't turn up, they'll be worried. Well, they ought to be.'

'Old Ferretface'll fob them off – tell them we went joyriding in the opposite direction.'

'Go on! If he's got any sense he's on his way back to Russia by now! When we get back and tell 'em—'

'Wish we were back now!'

There was little comfort in the prospect ahead. Jodie gained the fork and turned up the valley. There was nothing to be seen but the rain-swept hillsides under the low, black-bellied cloud, not even any more a comforting streak of sunset. If Nutty hadn't pinpointed the position of the hut while they waited they would never have seen it this time, but the headlights picked out a particular boulder and the thin walking track that left the road. When Jodie turned off the lights, they could see after their eyes became acclimatized the darker blob of the square hut against the featureless background. They all sat for a moment in silence, not wanting to get out.

'It might be locked.'

Hoomey, unexpectedly, found a torch down the side of the back seat. He switched it on and found it worked.

'I say, well *done*, Hoomey!' The others were fulsome in their praise, so that he suddenly felt less useless. They all had a cast round for anything else useful but only came up with a London street map and a packet of jelly babies, neither of which seemed likely to improve the night ahead. Reluctantly they piled out and started up the hillside in single file, John Pike leading with the torch. They were extraordinarily ill-clothed for the conditions, in their best black patent-leather shoes. The girls only had white blouses and black skirts, not even comfortable jeans, and they were all soaked through by the time they had slipped and slithered up the peat-slimy path. The door opened on a latch.

They piled in.

Hoomey swooshed the torch round. 'Cor, we're in luck!'

It was a climbers' bothy, made from an old stalking lodge, and better maintained than most. It was clean and dry and had a fireplace with cut wood stacked beside it and, on a stone ledge above, some old stumps of candle and two tins of baked beans.

'Matches?'

They were all soaked and shivering. The torch searched furiously.

'There's the cigarette lighter in the car,' Jodie said. 'It might light one of the candles.'

'Let's have a look first.'

There was an old cupboard with a few more relics in it: a nearly empty bottle of tomato ketchup, some paperback thrillers . . . a box of matches! Jodie opened it and found it full of used duds.

'Oh, no!'

She emptied it on the earth floor and scratched over them, triumphantly surfacing with one unused match.

'How's that for luck!'

'Light a candle!'

'No, wait,' Christian said. 'It's a fire we want. We must get it ready first. Before the candle.'

John Pike started tearing pages out of the paperbacks. The stacked wood was in fairly thick logs and there was little tinder, but some of it was birch and Christian started tearing off streamers of bark.

'Keep the torch still, Hoomey!'

Nutty was impressed. 'You trained as Boy Scouts or something?'

'We do survival training at school. Try and get some splinters off the logs. You've got good fingernails.'

Arnold reckoned he was a survivor, but this country was something different. He could not stop shaking and thought he was going to pass out.

Nutty thought survival training was a much better subject than home economics and wished her dim school offered it. She thought poor Arnie looked like death and Christian not much better, white and shaking with his stiff-upper-lip reticence, not complaining. John Pike was like a steadfast terrier, always ready to beaver away or stand firm, as the case required. Funny how being in trouble showed up people's characters. Christian must have gone in after Arnie without even thinking of the risk, and who was Arnie to him? Not as if he was his brother or something. Imagine Hoomey doing such a thing! And herself, come to that. Jodie, cool, calm and aggressive, was tearing at the logs with her violinist's pared-down nails already showing blood. The torchlight was trembling violently in Hoomey's hand – poor little Hoomey, who only asked for a quiet life and didn't seem to get it!

With such total concentration beamed on the creation of fire, there was no way the single match could fail to get a result. After a heart-stopping, damp splutter, it raised enough energy to set alight page one hundred and ten of Jeffrey Archer's *Not a Penny More, Not a Penny Less* which was then applied to one, and then all of the candle stumps. Whole chapters of literature were then lit in the fireplace, the smallest log propped behind and the tinder fed into the flames. The logs, being of pine and birch, and dry, took light without any trouble. John Pike piled on more and the crackling flames were soon roaring up the chimney.

It was amazing how quickly their spirits revived. They crouched round, steaming, the smell of hot wet wool filling their nostrils. Sparks flew; round black holes soon spattered their best clothes. John Pike burst the top of the bean tins by battering them with stones, and they propped them to warm by the flames.

Arnie was pushed to the front, to the hottest spot, and felt himself reviving, in spite of an almighty headache.

'He knocked me stupid with a spanner or something. And when we were driving along, every time I moved he gave me another clonk. By the time we got to the bridge I was all groggy.

I thought I was going over a cliff. I thought I was dead.'

'You've got as many lives as a cat, Arnie,' said John Pike.

'What're we going to do next?' Nutty asked. 'They'll all be searching for us madly. We ought to put out signals! We got to spend the night here?'

'Think of somewhere better! You can go and make signals to your heart's content, but leave me out of it.' Christian, steaming, could not stop yawning. 'I'm going to bed down for a few hours. Wait till the rain stops. We can go down when it gets light.'

'D'you think they'll put out a search-party?'

'Only if they know we're missing. The Turkins have probably told 'em we got a lift home with someone. Or they would take us in their Citroen. It's big enough. Being friends of Boris. I wouldn't put it past them.'

'Oh!' Nutty's face dropped. She fancied being searched for by helicopter and, with luck, being swung aboard on the end of a rope like you saw on the television. She got up and went over to the window that looked down the valley. It was still raining hard. She pressed her burning forehead against the glass and looked out into the darkness. There was nothing to be seen, not even a rim of horizon against the sky – only . . . She stiffened, stared.

She tried to sound cool, like Jodie. 'You know what?'

'What?' they said to humour her.

'Someone's coming!'

'What do you mean?' Christian woke up abruptly.

'Headlights coming up the valley.'

They all rushed to the window to look. Far away, the way they had come earlier, still far in the distance, two sets of headlights could be seen approaching.

'Oh good!' cried Hoomey, thinking of his warm bed and cups of tea and more chocolate cake. 'They've found us!'

Not all the others seemed to share his enthusiasm.

'Who's found us? That's the question,' Christian said quietly.

In the crush, Arnold found himself suddenly feeling queasy again.

'You don't mean—?'

'Might be just gamekeepers or something,' Jodie said hopefully.

'It might be,' Christian agreed. But his voice was subdued. Then, 'They're a funny lot, Boris's keepers. Persistent. I don't think it would be wise to run and meet them, waving our arms.'

'Blockade the door!' Nutty decided.

'Wait and see.'

The fire no longer seemed to give out the same cheer. It fell into embers and its bright light died. Arnie went back to it with what sounded suspiciously like a sob – a gulp, at least – (after all, it was him they were after) and the General's disquiet infected all the others. Nutty's enthusiasm faded.

'You think it – it really is – them?'

'We'll soon find out.'

Slowly but steadily, occasionally lurching out of sight, but always reappearing, the two sets of headlights moved towards them up the valley.

CHAPTER NINE

Nobody said much. Mildred's car blocked the track below the bothy and there was no way round it, but no-one offered to go and move it.

Christian walked back to the fire and stood silently looking into its cheerful flames. He knew he was the natural leader and knew that he had got them all into this jam. But he had saved Arnold. So far so good. But he did not like what he was thinking now. He was thinking that Boris's keepers were a ruthless lot and were no doubt wishing the six interfering kids could be wiped off the face of the earth. How? If they didn't have a plan, why were they coming? Why were they persisting?

He felt afraid, and very tired. Blast Jodie for producing the troublesome Arnold! Yet Christian admired Arnold's resilience; he was like a rubber ball, bouncing back from disaster with his hair sticking up ever more briskly, his beady dark eyes alert for the next sniff of danger. No-one could accuse him of being a whinger.

John Pike joined him presently.

'What if it's them?'

Christian knew John Pike knew, but the girls still thought it was a lark. Hoomey was useless but Arnold a born fighter.

'Bad.' He shrugged.

'They can't murder six of us. Bit over the top,' John Pike said, and grinned.

'I bet they'd like to. They've got a grand living ahead of them, if nobody knows. Boris is world class. You think about it.'

'Rather not actually.'

'Exactly.'

'We could keep 'em out. Barricade the door.'

'Yeah, I was thinking that. There'll be a search party for us eventually, if we can hang on.'

There was only the one door which could easily be kept shut with a large log shoved against it, wedged under its cross-timbering. A large log was to hand, in the shape of a makeshift bench balanced on a couple of rocks beside the fire.

Christian went back to the window and looked out. The lights were now quite close, having passed the track down to the Falls. It could be a couple of innocent parties going up the valley – the track obviously led somewhere . . .

Christian savoured for a moment the relief he would feel if that proved the case.

The lights halted. In the headlights Mildred's car showed up, blocking the way. The watchers held their breath.

'The keys are still in it. They can move it, if they want to go on.'

The person driving the first car got out and went back to the second car. After he had crossed the beam of the headlights they couldn't see what was happening, but presumably they were talking.

'Hush! Listen!' Christian commanded.

After about half a minute there came the sound of car doors slamming. Then the headlights were extinguished.

'They're coming!'

'Get that bench!'

They manhandled the hefty log into place, jamming it hard against the door and wedging its heel into the earth floor as best they could.

'That'll hold them.'

The rain had eased off and in the half-gloaming of the Northern night they knew the hut was visible. No doubt too the firelight showed through the windows. There were only two windows, both small, and with fixed glass. Christian turned the beam of Mildred's torch through one of the windows and picked them out – Ferretface and the two Turkins approaching like tanks over the hinterland.

They were all very tense: even Nutty's adrenalin could not spark any witticisms in the face of this relentless pressure. Nobody could work out what they intended to do. They couldn't murder all six of them! Could they . . . ? Hoomey made some faint squeaking noises and turned away. Arnold tried not to feel as if someone had hit him on the head with a spanner and thrown him over a waterfall, but found it very difficult. He could not stop himself trembling.

Christian kept the full beam on them as they came to the door. Ferretface tried to open it and found he couldn't. He thumped a few times and then turned to Mrs Turkin. They conferred.

'We wish to talk with you! Let us in!' Mrs Turkin shouted.

They were all crowded round the two windows to watch, with the torchbeam steady on the trio. Their respective faces were no more attractive in the dusk and the rain than they had ever been, nutcracker faces with angry mouths and hard eyes – hatchet faces, whose physiognomy traced back to Genghis Khan or worse. Manipulators of the unfortunate Boris, who was a really nice guy. Boris needed rescuing as much as Arnold, Christian thought, as he made his reply.

'No deal! You can talk from there.'

'We don't want to talk to you!'

'*Shut up, Nutty!*'

'You do not understand us! We wish to explain.'

'Explain from there.'

After a few moments discussion Ferretface applied his bulky form to the door but it held easily.

'Very cold out here. We wish to talk!'

Christian was relieved how easily their defence held off the attack and knew they had the upper hand. The door was very strongly built and the bench massive against it. He stood watching them, still holding the torch in his hand.

Suddenly, to his amazement, Mr Turkin, the shadowy background one of the three, stepped forward and levelled a revolver straight at him.

'Open the door!'

'It's a toy gun!' Nutty shouted. 'Bet you!'

'Don't fall for it, Chris,' John Pike. 'It's just a trick.'

The next moment there was a sharp explosion and the window glass shattered. Christian jumped back, dropping the torch, and instantly there was another crack and the toy gun let rip into the top of his arm with a bite that made him scream out.

'You let us in!' Mrs Turkin roared. 'Or we keel you all!'

'Chris, are you OK?'

137

They thought he was dead, about to sway and fall like a cowboy actor. John Pike leapt to his side. Christian found that he was still very much alive, but shaking with anger more than fright.

'It missed – of course I'm all right!' He let out some fearful oaths that the girls had never dreamed he knew and then said, 'Let them in, for goodness sake, they mean business!'

His arm burned like fire and he could feel the blood running down inside his best orchestra jersey, but it didn't feel like an artery or bone, only flesh – as far as he could tell, never having been shot before. He had had hurts worse than this though, and never screamed out. He was furiously angry, his pride and his plans smashed simultaneously.

The shooting seemed to have enraged Mrs Turkin equally, for she was berating her husband like a virago out in the rain. Even if they could not understand what she was saying, the gist was very clear. She was still at it as they opened the door.

Mr Turkin, taking no notice of her, swung the revolver round at them and gestured them all up one end of the room. They went, very cautiously. Turkin picked up the torch and shone it on them.

'You keep steel,' said Mrs Turkin, switching her vitriolic gaze from her companion to them.

'You no trouble!' She jabbed the torch at Christian. 'You – you keep quiet.'

Then she switched her nagging attention back to the two men. They neither of them changed their expressions at all. Ferretface went over to the fire and stood in front of it, looking into the flames. Then he put some more wood on it and the fresh pine crackled up with a roar and spat out sparks. Ferretface brushed them off his trousers.

'Hope he goes up in smoke,' said Nutty.

They all sat along the wall, in a row, watching the revolver. There was safety in numbers but they didn't feel very safe. The revolver shots had made everything quite different. Nutty could see a large patch of blood on Christian's upper arm, which he was holding with his other hand. He was very white.

'You can't kill all of us!' John Pike said suddenly, sounding rather cross. 'What are you going to do next?'

'We stay 'ere and you keep quiet, or we 'urt you.'

They put the big log back to its use as a bench and sat on it in front of the fire, muttering between themselves. The man with the gun was turned in their direction, watching them, and the gun was still in his hand. They all muttered together, apparently in argument. The woman seemed to be the boss, or at least was the most outspoken, and her 'husband' with the gun was the quietest. But his silence had an ominous weight. One had the feeling that, if he wanted, he could toss off the lady's vituperation with a shrug like shaking off a fly, and she would be quiet.

Nutty christened her Navratilova. 'She's got a big serve. Wham!' Nutty could not believe, in spite of Christian's arm, that any harm could come to them.

'Fort Knox'll be over soon in a helicopter,' she said to Hoomey. 'Stop sniffling.'

Ferretface gave the impression of being subservient, perhaps just a hired 'heavy', the one who murdered the first Mr Turkin no doubt, and who had been directed to wipe out Arnold. He had never been seen with the musical set, but only in the chauffeur's job. Perhaps he kept tabs on Boris. Where was Boris? By now, they assumed, their friends would all be home and dry, tucking into supper. A nice thought.

The bothy was now warm and snug and when the Russian trio told them all to lie down and go to sleep the idea seemed quite attractive. Better than being lined up against the wall and shot, which alternative had been in all their minds. Better to be killed in the morning, fresh and alert . . . should sleep come, which it did quite quickly to Hoomey and Arnold, less quickly to the girls and not at all to Christian. His arm had stopped bleeding but the shock and the throbbing pain seemed to have fixed in his brain rather than in his body.

John Pike, who knew his dilemma, said, 'It's not your fault how it turned out.'

'No?'

It had all been a lark, hiding Arnold, when in fact it wasn't at all, and they should have turned it over to their teachers straight away. Especially after Arnold's night in the ballroom. But Christian had wanted to get on with the music: he saw his mistake now – not wanting his good time interrupted. Being irresponsible. Christian's upbringing had been all about being responsible. John Pike knew Christian's burdens, having stayed with him during the holidays a few times.

'They can't kill us all, for goodness sake!'

They kept telling themselves that. The waterfall would get a blockage.

The Russians kept the fire going, sitting muttering between themselves for some time, then stretching out to sleep in the best spot in front of the hearth – but always with one of them awake, gun at the ready. They seemed quite prepared to accept the hardship of the bothy in the pursuit of their goal: they were an iron-hard bunch, the lady included.

Some time during the night the rain stopped, the stars came out and the wind died down. It started coming light early and for once, when there was very little to look forward to, the day was full of promise.

John Pike woke and went outside for a pee. Ferretface followed him with the gun and leaned in the doorway. John Pike had no illusions about getting away: if he ran for it, he knew the man would shoot him. He looked out down the valley and saw a warm mist lying, the hillsides glittering, a trio of deer on the far hillside watching, then moving off with effortless grace up over the tops. They got shot too. He watched them, trying to get the feel of this strange new day. Below on the track the three cars stood one behind the other: Mildred's old Cortina, the Citroen and a rather battered van.

As there was no dressing to do and no breakfast to cook, getting ready to go took no time at all. They went out into the day stiffly, urged by Ferretface's revolver. Arnold appeared to have recovered from his experiences of the day before, but Christian's arm was stiff and swollen and he felt only half there – and that reluctantly. They slithered down the track, shivering in the bright air, and were herded into the back of the battered van. The door behind them was shut and locked, and Ferretface came round and got in the driving seat. Mrs Turkin got in beside him, with the revolver.

They had all expected that the cars would turn round and go back the way they had come, and were surprised when Mr Turkin drove the Cortina off the track out of the way, got back in the Citroen and started off to continue up the valley. Ferretface started the van and followed. The road was very bad, full of potholes, and progress slow, and none of them could work out where it could possibly be leading.

'Perhaps they're just going to dump us?' Jodie suggested.

'Oh, great! I like hiking!' said Arnold.

'Better than swimming?'

Christian couldn't work it out. However far they travelled in the cars to be dumped, they could get back to civilization, surely? The cars could hardly take them into so remote an area that they could not find a way back. The track was climbing and the motors were in low gear, having a rough time. Ahead there seemed to be a saddle between the steep hillsides on either side: the track disappeared over the top and the horizon beyond that was far distant. The top, when they arrived, appeared to be another sort of beauty spot, no doubt for the view, for there was car parking scraped out on one side and the track from there on was only for walkers.

Both cars pulled into the car park.

Ferretface and Mrs Turkin got out, slamming their doors behind them. Ferretface stood by his door with the revolver, while Mrs Turkin went to confer with her husband.

'Hm, nice view,' Nutty commented. 'Pity there's not a hotdog van.'

'I'm dying of hunger!' Hoomey wailed.

Better than dying of something else, more quickly, Christian thought. He didn't like the look of it. He caught John Pike's eye and turned away. Nothing to say. They were all locked into a valueless van on the edge of a precipice. Had Hoomey not noticed? No. Jodie was actually combing her hair with a comb out of her skirt pocket. Christian groaned.

'Your arm hurting?' Nutty asked.

He couldn't reply.

Mr Turkin nodded to Ferretface who got back into the driving seat. He still had the revolver, which he put on the dashboard. He leaned over and fiddled with the passenger door lock, and then started the engine again. He drove out of the car park and, more or less, into the view. The ground fell away beneath them in a great sweep of scree to the lip of a deep gorge, no doubt a cousin of the one they had encountered the day before, only lower down the valley and bigger and better than higher up. A few battered trees clung here and there to the scree and way below them tops of trees stuck up above the lip of the gorge, showing how deep it was. There was no path down to it and no doubt few people went down.

They were going down, Christian knew. Like into a deep hole, their remains not to be found for days.

It still hadn't dawned on the others, only John Pike.

'Oh no!' he whispered.

He looked at Christian, who recognized the appeal: he, the General's son, had to think of a way out of this, or else. There wasn't a way.

The Turkins had turned the Citroen round to go back, and were waiting with the engine running for Ferretface.

He had his door open now. He reached for his revolver, let off the handbrake, put the car in gear and jumped out. As he went he slammed the door behind him. The old van took off, found the incline to its liking and plunged down like a horse let out in a field.

Christian had a glimpse of Nutty's face – her expression of unbelieving horror. Hoomey began to scream. Jodie dropped her comb.

'Drive it!' said John Pike. 'For heaven's sake, Chris, drive it!'

He crashed his shoulder against the back door but it was resolutely locked.

Nutty stood up and started to beat her fists against the side as if she could batter them in. Christian shoved past her and started to climb into the front seats, which was difficult. John Pike bunked him from behind.

'The brake! The handbrake!'

Christian reached for it and hauled it up, but the van still kept going – it made scarcely any difference. The slope was a bare sheet of small grit, which just moved down inexorably under the gripped wheels. From the front seat Christian had a clear view of an uninterrupted slide to total disaster – the lip of the gorge and the tops of the fir trees on the far side just showing. There seemed to be no trees on their side which might possibly break their fall. And it was a long fall, into a maelstrom of water in flood – he knew it only too well.

John Pike was leaning over, trying to open the passenger door, but it would not give, locked in some way which he could not find. The van was going too fast now to make opening the window any sort of an option. It bounced and swayed and in the back they started to get thrown off balance. Low gear made no difference to their relentless progress, the land steepening and their speed increasing. The old van started to sway alarmingly.

'Steer it, Chris – sideways!'

'It'll turn over!'

'Not too suddenly. Try it.'

Chris eased the wheel so that the tyres slewed on the gritty slope. There was a strong smell of burning rubber. The van lurched horribly. Everyone in the back screamed.

'Get the weight on this side!'

John Pike had grabbed Arnold by the arm, pulling him to the upside of the van. The girls scrabbled to follow. It was sailing dinghy practice, but made very little difference.

Christian, afraid the van would turn over, straightened it out again. But he could see that to turn across the slope was their only chance. And time was running out. The van was gathering momentum as the land fell away. He eased the wheel round again.

The vehicle lurched violently and, with great deliberation, still hurtling downhill, fell over on its side, and then on its roof. Inside they were flung up and over like washing in a tumble drier, a mix of soft body and hard metal, painful ... crunch, jab, crack ... no knowing where was what. Christian had a glimpse of the lip of the gorge out of a window that seemed to face the sky, and heard a tearing, scraping noise of metal on rock: then a tree in his vision, branches against white clouds. He thought he had died.

There was a smell of burning rubber again, and petrol, strongly. The engine had stopped, the grating gravel noise had stopped. There was a dripping noise and human groaning.

But there had been no fall. Christian couldn't work out which way up he was or what had happened, but felt, somehow, a slight swaying, as if he lay in a hammock. He instinctively did not move, only his eyes, looking.

It took some time to take stock, mainly because he was underneath John Pike, who was either dead or unconscious. Christian determined that the van was on its side, the driver's side; he lay against the door with John Pike on top of him. Out of the driver's window he could see branches, not big ones, only twigs, and out of the far side window there was nothing but sky. A bird was passing, it looked like a buzzard, with frazzled wing tips. In any other situation he would have been keenly interested.

He managed to push himself up on one elbow, in spite of the pain in his upper arm. It mattered to see who was dead and who was alive. From the twittering, whimpering, sighing noises behind him the omens were good: no actual screaming, nor dead silence either. Also, John Pike was breathing, he ascertained as he tried to manoeuvre out from under him – no mean feat under the circumstances. The swaying sensation came again, which – for some reason – he found very frightening.

He sat up, on the door, and looked down. What he saw nearly made him pass out.

He was looking straight down into the gorge. Far far below a white stream roared down between the rock cliffs with ten times the vigour he had withstood in his rescue the day before, sending up a white spray that hung over the abyss like mist. Immediately below him the ground fell sheer. But underneath the van, on the very lip of the chasm, there appeared to be a sort of rocky knob, with one puny alder tree growing out of the cup of earth that had collected in the rock's lee. It was this that had stopped the van's roll to destruction. The van was balanced – hence the swaying sensation – against the trunk of a slender tree holding on to a crevice in a large rock, above a forty-metre straight drop to certain death.

Christian shut his eyes. It was too awful to contemplate.

He heard Jodie's voice, shrill, 'Let's get out of here!'

'Don't move!' he yelled. 'Nobody move!'

Just when he needed him most, John Pike was not available, damn him. John Pike was the steady, the sheet anchor, the one to think of a way forward. Without him, Christian had to fight down panic and sheer terror. The others couldn't see what he could see. He tried to keep his voice calm.

'Jodie, don't move! Nobody move! The van is balanced on a tree trunk over the drop. If you move it might tip off. Just lie still. Is anybody hurt, Jodie?'

'I'm not.'

'Nor me,' said Nutty, somewhat dubiously.

'Arnie's cracked his head. It's bleeding and he's all dopey.'

'I think Hoomey's died of fright,' said Nutty.

'No. He's breathing. Complaining again, Hoomey? You're not dead so don't worry. Just keep still. General's orders.'

A whimpering noise indicated that Hoomey was taking notice.

'Where are we?'

'Don't ask,' said Jodie. 'Can't we even sit up?'

'If we never move,' Nutty said, 'and nobody finds us, where does that get us?'

'One at a time, try getting comfortable. But don't shift the balance. Very, very carefully.'

It was true they had to help themselves. Things might be better than he knew.

'Jodie first.'

The sickening, slight swaying proved the importance of his warnings more than any words. Once they recognized the situation they acted with commendable calm and sense; it was, after all, a matter of life and death. One only had to look. When they came upright they too, could look down into the gaping abyss below.

They sat, eventually, in a row on the driver side of the van, which was their floor. Through the window was the dreadful view, but only Christian and Jodie, sitting nearest, could see it properly. Nutty, having had a white-faced glimpse, made sure Hoomey was at the back. John Pike was still unconscious and Arnold too groggy to take any interest.

'Now what?' said Nutty quietly.

They had made the casualties as comfortable as they could, and hoped they would shortly come round. They had no visible signs of damage, beyond Arnold's graze on the temple. John Pike's colour wasn't bad and he was making stirring signs.

'Do you think they watched?' Jodie said. 'Or drove away?'

'They were driving away,' Christian said. 'With luck they never saw. They think we went over.'

He was trying the window handle, to see if he could open the window. It was like a trap-door into the gorge.

Jodie said, 'If people come up here to look at the view, from that car park, they'll see us and come down. We'll get rescued.'

'It wasn't well-used,' Nutty pointed out. 'I bet on a day like this nobody comes.'

'It's a walking area. Walkers might come.'

On the far side of the gorge Christian could see

a track following the contour halfway up the cliff, which was presumably a walkers' track. It wasn't so sheer on the far side. Just their luck. Beneath them the rock fell away vertically to a ledge about eight metres below. Below the ledge there was a possible way down, though very steep. They were all wearing hopeless shoes.

At least they were still alive. Christian put his head back and closed his eyes, trying to take stock. He was in no state to make decisions, but he had to. They could be a very long time waiting to be rescued. It wasn't in their natures not to try, he knew.

Jodie said, 'If we had a rope we could get down.'

'Yeah.' But there wasn't a rope. The van was quite bare.

'We could tear our clothes in strips and make a rope,' said Nutty.

Christian thought they would all die of cold before a good enough rope could be produced. None of them had a knife and Nutty, although she tried with her skirt, could not even get started ripping it up. The hems were too tough.

'And by the time you've knotted it together – the knots take up most of the stuff anyway. How come people do it in books?'

'They use sheets.'

'Ah, well, sheets'd be OK. But we haven't got any.'

Christian tried standing up, opening the window the other side that looked to the sky, but it was jammed, nor could he move the door. The only way out was through the trapdoor window beside him. If he lay down and hung Hoomey out at arm's length, Hoomey might just drop the last seven or so metres to the ledge. Might. Too risky. Hoomey wouldn't, anyway. Jodie might. Christian did not suggest it. Nutty was getting restless.

'We can't just sit here!'

'Don't jump about, for goodness sake!'

They could all go anyway, if the little tree gave up or the boulder slipped.

'We might just *have* to sit here,' he said wearily. His shot arm was throbbing painfully and he didn't feel like a leader of men any more. Fortunately John Pike was beginning to make signs of returning to consciousness. Christian persuaded him not to leap to his feet and John Pike took in the situation with a quite natural amazement. He lay looking at the square of sky above his head, taking it in.

'If you really tried, you couldn't get yourself in a fix like this! It's pure chance.'

'Good luck, strictly speaking.'

Even turning over on to his side, John Pike could feel the delicacy of the truck's balancing act. He looked out of the trap-door, considering.

'Just a chance . . . '

'What?'

'You could drop on to that ledge without carrying on down.'

'I wouldn't like to do it.'

'No. Nor would I.'

'The best chance is somebody coming along that track across the other side and seeing us. Or from above, but we can't see what's happening up there.'

'Navratilova's probably on her way down to give us a push,' Nutty said. 'How the hell do they expect to get away with it?'

'Nobody knows about what they did last night, only us. Nobody will connect them with our disappearance,' Jodie said.

'They'll all think we went joy-riding. Mildred'll think so, the way we all dropped her harp and tore off in her car.'

Blue sky was opening up in their view, with huge white clouds sailing along. A wind was rising, tossing the tops of the fir trees below. Christian did not like to remark on it, but he could feel the van reacting to the buffeting of the wind. It was so tender, a good blast could well finish them. Sitting still doing nothing was the hardest of all their options.

'Look,' said John Pike. 'On the track.'

Christian held his breath. Over the horizon

where the track wound out of sight towards the upper moors, a file of horses and riders could be seen coming down. They would pass directly across the valley in front of them.

'They're bound to see us!'

'They might think we're an old accident – we need to send out a signal—'

'A shirt – a blouse – wave it!'

'White'll show up! Come on, Hoomey, strip off! It's time you helped!'

Nutty bullied Hoomey into taking off his shirt. She tore it off over his head and passed it up to Christian. Christian hung it out of the window and waved it backwards and forwards.

'Passing ships,' said Nutty. 'S'like being on a desert island.'

'Suppose they don't look!'

'Oh, go on, they're tourists! Looking at the view is what it's all about.'

'People like gruesome accidents. That's what we are.'

'Not yet we're not.'

It helped to talk rubbish, rather than think about the sickly, faint shivering of the poised van. Nutty could feel the cold sweat of fear sticky between her shoulder-blades. Sitting still waiting was the most difficult act of all.

The file of horses moved on for some time, then the leader halted. It was too far away to see what he was doing, but Christian saw an arm point in their direction. He passed this information back, waving the shirt more vigorously. Then the horses moved on, but at a much faster pace. They moved out of the picture. Christian couldn't see them any more and gave Hoomey his shirt back.

'It looks hopeful.'

It helped a lot; good for morale, Christian thought, but he still didn't see how they were going to be saved without a fatigue party of Royal Engineers who probably weren't around. Horses usually meant women, and the most he allowed himself to expect was that they would go for help, which would take hours. The wind was rising all the time: for once it was a glorious day, the great white clouds whizzing overhead against a sky of purest blue. Life was very desirable, Christian thought, with a sick shudder. He had never been in such a mess before.

Arnold had come round but wasn't happy.

'I'm starving!'

Nobody told him he was perched in a tree halfway down a precipice. It didn't seem worthwhile. He might want to look, which would tip the balance. Jodie told him to lie still because he was concussed.

They waited.

Even if they were coming to help, the riders had

to cross the river in spate, probably impossible.

They played I Spy, which wasn't riveting. Christian thought of D for Death but didn't say. Then they had a sort of quiz which Jodie organized. Hoomey started to cry. Nutty rounded on him and told him he wasn't even fit to play the triangle. John Pike, as head percussionist, defended the triangle and they had a quarrel, which Nutty cut off by saying she was dying to have a pee.

'You'll have to wet your knickers then! Don't move,' Christian said.

He had a nasty feeling that the van was slipping infinitesimally, because he could see more out of the window below him than he could earlier. While he was trying to check on this a movement caught his eye. Emerging from the gorge was a single figure. It was making in their direction but had a daunting climb ahead of it. It seemed to be carrying something on its back.

He reported back. The atmosphere changed immediately. Hoomey stopped crying and Nutty said she would hang on.

Whoever their rescuer was, it was some climber, Christian established. Not a horsey woman; it could only be a professional mountain man by the ease and speed of movement. Christian felt better and better by the minute as he watched. He kept up a running commentary and everyone started to get very excited.

'Has he got a rope?'

'I think he has. He's got something anyway.'

'Wings!'

He appeared to be a man of about forty, lean and hard, wearing riding boots and breeches. He came up steadily until he was within shouting distance below, when he stopped and looked up.

'How many of you in that thing?'

'Six of us!'

He swore quite heartily and shouted up, 'Don't any of you move!'

As if we didn't know, thought Christian.

Christian could now see that what he carried on his back was a load of stirrup leathers. Brilliant! Buckled together and really strong, they would be better than a rope.

The man gained the little ledge, his point of no return, and put down the stirrup leathers.

He looked up. 'Very dicey,' he called up conversationally. 'I can see it swaying from here. I think if we don't get you out, the wind'll push it off before proper help comes. You need a helicopter to hold it, ideally.'

He made it sound as if it was all in a day's work to come across such a problem – no time wasted asking how they got in such a situation, no panics. Christian was flooded with a ridiculous joy at such a man taking over. He had thought it was bound to be some idiot who wanted to help but would have no idea how to go about it. This man had taken a reel of thread out of his pocket and was tying a small rock to the end. He unravelled it and tied the other end to one of the stirrup leathers, which he then proceeded to buckle together.

'I had a tack repair kit in my saddle-bag luckily. I could see what might be needed through my binoculars. Once you've caught the rock – try not to make any sudden movement . . . I'll try and aim it right into the window – pull it in very gently. It's pretty strong. Careful now.'

He made sure it was coiled correctly and would run, and then stood taking aim. It was tricky, as the narrowness of the ledge meant he had to throw virtually straight up. But, as Christian felt himself shivering with nerves at the importance of catching it, it came flying up right into his outstretched hand, and he caught it first go.

'Pull it in and fix the first leather round the seat bearer.'

It was long enough, ending about two metres above the ledge.

The man tested it by putting his weight on it. It was in the centre of the truck's precarious balance, which was phenomenal luck. The man then looked up and said, 'The rest is up to you, matey. I suggest you send the lightest first.'

He lit a cigarette and took a deep inhalation. He didn't think they might all make it.

Nor did Christian, now it came to the point. To move the girls along – and Christian had been brought up to believe, quite rightly, it was women and children first – it meant balancing the movement by sending someone back to compensate. This role was accepted without even talking about it by John Pike.

'Jodie first. She's the lightest. Then Nutty, then Hoomey. Gently, Jodie—' He didn't have to say, they could all sense it. She was nearest, which helped. As she slid gingerly forward, John Pike edged back. To go down would take courage, especially the first, but Christian knew she would. Hoomey might be different. She wriggled over him and turned on to her front, putting her legs out into space. Christian saw that she was terrified. So was he.

'Good girl.'

He took her hands and let her down and transferred her hands one by one to the leather rope.

'OK!'

'Chris—!' She was white as a sheet.

'*You've got to!*'

There was no choice at all. She went, at first inch by inch and then with more confidence. The man caught her dangling body and guided her feet on to the ledge. She looked up, radiant.

'It's easy! Tell Nutty—!'

The man made her climb down, sideways, so that she was out of the way – out of the way of the van should it fall, Christian noted silently. Nutty was protesting that Hoomey should go before her.

'He's lighter, and he won't go without me to bully him.'

She was right, Christian did not argue.

'Come on, you little rat!'

But Hoomey rose to the occasion, so desperate was he to regain terra firma. He disappeared with a squeal and a rush, making the van sway horribly. They gritted their teeth and even Nutty made no comment. She crawled forward in time with John Pike moving back. The success of the first two made it easier and she was the bravest of the bunch, Christian knew. He even managed to grin at her glittering expression as she departed down the rock face.

Arnold was a worry, his bang on the head and his late experiences not having improved his strength and determination. But his sense of self-preservation, always strong, overcame his weakness. He disappeared out of the hole and slid precariously down. He joined the other three sitting in a row on a ledge of tufty grass. Christian heard Jodie laugh. He didn't feel like laughing himself.

'You next.'

John Pike looked at him from the back of the van.

'You're nearer.'

'No. You.'

John didn't argue then. He crawled forward and Christian slithered back. He got into position on the leather rope and dropped over the edge. The van swayed alarmingly.

'Chris, you—'

'Oh, shut up! Go!'

Christian lay on the side of the van, the hole to safety now some four feet beyond his outstretched fingertips. He felt all the fight go out of his body suddenly, alone. He was scared rigid. He knew when he went forward the van would go. He could feel it slipping even now, and heard some stones grinding ominously against the side. The twigs and leaves were trembling against the sky and there was a soft, almost inaudible sigh of tearing roots.

A sharp voice came from below.

'Get out!'

It was almost as if he was paralysed. Too paralysed to die. Very, very slowly the van started to move.

He had to go then. He went out of the window headfirst, just as the window slid outwards away from its anchor. The little tree gave way and keeled outwards. Christian caught the swinging rope with one hand, held himself for a fraction of a moment and then let go as the van came over the cliff above him. He fell vertically and saw the great bulk of the van blot out the wonderful sunshine over his head, heard screaming, but knew it wasn't his. He just thought, this is dying, and a terrible regret.

The van fell down into the gorge with a frightening impact, tearing trees and rocks aside in its path, bouncing up and paraboling down like a live thing until it hit the rocks in the river and exploded. The roar echoed between the rock walls. Christian heard it, much to his surprise. He was still falling, but the van had missed him. He couldn't believe his luck, in spite of the fact that he was still rolling and bouncing himself, hitting ground at intervals with painful force. He made grabs as he went, at turf, at bushes, at rocks, mostly to little avail, but eventually, still some way above the river, he slammed up against a tree which was well bedded in and stopped with great suddenness. His body swung round and down and was about to take off again when his scrabbling fingers caught a solid root. Gripping hard, he braced himself, digging in, heels and elbows, almost with his teeth, hearing the awful booming of the water below which was leaping to receive him. Black fumes from the burning van stung his nostrils. But he held on and was still, at last, a crumpled survivor of a very nasty accident.

CHAPTER TEN

The horses were grazing by the side of the track with their riders chatting, sitting on the bank. They were on holiday, trail-riding across Scotland. Not having expected to meet such drama, they watched curiously as their leader returned at last with a string of six weary survivors. A certain euphoria at being alive had sustained them on the scramble down the cliff-face but when they reached the bridge – the same that Arnold had been tossed over the night before – and saw the horses waiting they slumped visibly. They flung themselves down on the grass in varying degrees of exhaustion. The two girls, not having been knocked out or otherwise injured, were in the best shape; John Pike and Arnold felt extremely groggy, and Christian was one throbbing, stumbling bruise on legs, not capable any longer of taking any sort of decision.

Fortunately their new leader, who appeared

to be called Tony, was a man to whom taking command came naturally. Christian suspected an army past. He was lean and fit and seemed to take difficulties in his stride. While they lay on the bank, he pieced together their extraordinary tale. The holiday riders nobly offered up their packed lunches and someone fetched tin mugfuls of water from the river, awed by the graphic account of injustice that had been perpetrated.

'We've got to catch 'em,' Nutty said, 'because if they hear we're not dead they'll be off like the wind. It's no good telephoning to say we're safe. They'll go as soon as they hear.'

'Nutty's right,' said John Pike. 'They could fly from Inverness down to Heathrow and be off while we're still getting back.'

Tony looked thoughtful.

'Can any of you ride?'

'I can,' said Nutty. 'I've got a show-jumper. And Christian plays polo.'

'I can ride,' Hoomey said, very quietly, so that no-one could hear him.

'We've got two spare horses,' Tony said. 'But no stirrup leathers, so we can't ride fast. If you two want to ride on ahead on the two spares – go down to that camping site and ring for the police, we'll follow on behind. There's a good track all the way.'

'It's the way we came up in the car.'

'The car's still up there, but it's out of petrol.'

Nutty looked at Christian, who was trying to kid himself that riding downhill, fast, bareback, was an easy option.

'Come on, Chris! The sooner we get the police—'

'I know.' Could he?

Tony said, 'It's up to you. We'll be along, but slowly. The other four can ride pillion.'

If Tony thought he could, presumably he could. Christian stood up. The two spare horses, grazing hard, were mean, lean beasts, not trekkers' plods at all. They wore headcollars, but Tony swapped them for bridles from two of the other horses. Nutty leapt forward eagerly, hitching up her orchestra skirt round her bottom and Tony gave her a leg up. Her sturdy brown legs surprised the grazing horse with a grip of iron and he pulled himself together smartly. Christian smiled. Tony gave him a leg-up on to the other horse.

He grinned and said, 'Tell yourself it must be better than walking!'

The two of them crossed the bridge and went up the other side at a fast canter, over the brow and out of sight.

'Now, the rest of you—'

Tony allocated the four others to a horse each, riding pillion. The saddles were hefty endurance saddles but, even so, small for two bottoms, not very comfortable. He took Arnold up behind him,

167

Arnold looking the groggiest of the four, and set off to follow the others, but at a mere walk.

Arnold laid his head gratefully against Tony's back. The world was going round and his head was full of cymbal clashes. The music seemed to be swilling through him, those great tunes flooding all his senses, and he saw himself standing up with a cymbal at the ready in each hand, listening to the pulsing crescendo as it rose up towards him, poised to crown it with his gorgeous crash. It seemed to go on and on, the crescendo, without ever reaching his moment, so that he went on standing there, cymbals at the ready. It seemed very strange, because when he opened his eyes there was no orchestra there at all, only huge white clouds racing across a deep blue sky. He had no idea where he could be, nor why he was on a horse. A *horse*? The rhythm of its stride was like the beat of John Pike's drum and the clink of shoe on stones like the tinkling of Hoomey's triangle. Arnold was on a horse, in an orchestra, looking at the sky, and smiling.

Jodie thought Arnold had passed out, but as he didn't seem to fall off there didn't seem any point in drawing attention to the fact. Her rider was an American who couldn't get over the sight of the van cartwheeling down the cliff and exploding in the gorge. He kept asking Jodie what they had been up to, but she was really too tired to tell him. When she tried to explain that they had been locked in and despatched to their certain deaths, it seemed such an unlikely story that she stopped in mid-telling, wondering if it hadn't all been some sort of a bad dream. But there they all were, in varying states of distress, still being rescued, when by rights they should have been concentrating on their music in the hall with the antlers round the wall. That's what the others would be doing now. She hoped they were being missed. Nutty and Hoomey apart, they were quite important members of the orchestra. Then she realized that, of course, they were being missed. The responsible Mrs Knox would be doing her nut at losing no less than five of her children. It was obviously gross carelessness on her part, after all her counting and double-checking. Jodie smiled at the thought that, having lost five, she was shortly going to find six. Poor little Arnie would stand revealed at last. Jodie then realized that she was sorry for Arnold, a brave and resourceful lad, who had no friends or relations to welcome him back, only a bleak room waiting somewhere in London, with a lock on the door. He deserved better. He played a good cymbal, better than Nutty. Nutty only did it for a lark. Arnold had done it with passion.

Their steady horses came up over the rise and they looked down the long valley home, but there was no sign of Nutty and Christian ahead of them.

As they galloped up the track Christian felt himself, for all his aches and pains, coming to, back into real life. It was nearly over, the long ordeal, the frights, the unwanted adventure, and after all the inevitable unravelling ahead of them, there was still a week of orchestra and a good time. He hadn't disgraced himself either, and Arnold, although battered, was safe. He had found out a lot, mostly about himself, and felt he knew what good friends were. For Nutty, the tank-shaped bundle of energy urging her horse on ahead of him, he had nothing but admiration. Not the sort of girl one would wish to take out, but a girl to rely on, a good friend, like John Pike. What his father would call a good egg.

He could see she was a strong and experienced rider: he had not expected it. He had ridden ever since he could remember and took it for granted but she lived in the middle of a town. He didn't see how. There were quite a lot of things he didn't see how, he realized, having had a problem-free life with all the good things. Arnold, for example . . . Christian did not know why he was philosophizing as he rode: possibly having just nearly died, all his past life was appearing before his eyes now, instead of when he was falling down the cliff. It hadn't happened then. Nothing so noble, merely blinding fear. He had been sick when he had stopped and had cried too, but there had been no-one to see. It didn't matter much about being brave if there was no-one to see. They had all so terribly nearly died it was no wonder his brain was now behaving in this rather odd and reflective fashion.

They came up over the rise and turned down the valley. Trotting bareback was not very comfortable; walking and cantering seemed the best options, and they soon found that the horses were very fit. They could keep up a loping canter for some time. On the rougher bits they walked, and the horses had a rest.

It was a long way down the valley, farther than they had remembered, and it was with relief that they at last came on to a better road and saw the camping site below them. In the bright sunshine it looked cheerful and active, the bright tents blooming on the grass like giant flowers, and a roof with Restaurant painted on it, which looked very good to the two hungry riders above. Mostly the tents had cars parked beside them but there was a small car park opposite the restaurant. There were three cars in it.

One of them was a black Citroen.

Christian reined in sharply. They were on a

hairpin bend, still above the site, and too far away to see the number plate.

'It can't be—!'

'How long since they shoved us over the cliff? It's ages, surely?'

'Yeah – but . . . they never slept last night, they were hungry, they were dirty, they had a lot to think about . . . they could have had showers here, fed, even had a nap in the sun . . . you think about it. It *is* possible. If they were to arrive back at the lodge all dirty and hungry, like they were, people would have been a bit surprised, wouldn't they?'

'I suppose so,' said Nutty, visibly sagging. Then she perked up. 'But they'll be going back to Boris, surely? We've only got to ring the police to catch them back there.'

'I suppose so.' Christian wasn't sure. His brain wasn't working very well any longer. He longed to hand his problems over to the police where they belonged.

'There's a phone box in the restaurant entrance. I can see it.'

Tony had given them phone money, in case more than 999 was needed.

'You hold the horses. I'll go and phone,' Nutty said.

'They might be in the restaurant. If they see you—!'

'They won't see me, I'll make sure.'

'Remember, your orchestra clothes – they'll recognize them in a flash.'

It was true, her black skirt, white(ish) blouse and tie stood out rather in the camping world of shorts and orange anoraks. She slid off her horse and handed the reins to Christian, who was very doubtful about the wisdom of the move. If she got through to the police though . . . he could relax.

'You watch, I'll do it very cleverly!'

She gave him her amazing grin and started off. She made a large detour below the road, where she wouldn't be seen, slithering through the heather. Christian, too, moved off below the road and found a useful declivity which made a good hiding place. He got off and watched Nutty, just his head sticking up over the heather. She came out below the car park, and took a yellow anorak that was blowing on a makeshift washing line and put it on over her blouse and jersey. Then she walked boldly into the café. Christian couldn't see her any more.

Nutty went into the phone booth. There were swing doors into the café and she could see the Turkins and Ferretface sitting at a table drinking coffee.

Her heart was thumping hard as she dialled 999. Coffee meant they had nearly finished.

'Police, Fire or Ambulance?'

173

'Police!' She was tempted to say everything.

'My name is Deirdre McTavish. I think I am a missing person. I am talking from—' God, she had no idea where she was! She looked at the telephone number on the dial and read it out. 'It's a camping site half way up a mountain somewhere—' Flash of inspiration! '—on the way to Antrim Falls.'

They were getting up from the table! Mrs Turkin was walking firmly towards the doors, while the other two lingered. Right beside the telephone booth was a door marked Ladies. Nutty turned her head towards the wall and hunched down into the voluminous (Large Man's) anorak. It was very wet which she hadn't noticed when she took it. Mrs Turkin swung through the restaurant doors, past the telephone booth and into the ladies. The telephone booth had no doors, only a sort of hood thing.

'A black Citroen will be driving down shortly and you've got to stop them! They tried to kill us. They pushed us over a gorge!'

'Are you the lot from the Youth Orchestra, that went joy-riding?'

'Yes, but we didn't go joy-riding. We were abducted. And the people that did it . . . '

She dropped her voice as Mr Turkin and Ferretface came out of the restaurant and stood waiting for their female accomplice. They were about three metres away. Ferretface was lighting a cigarette.

'This black Citroen – what's its number?'

Nutty could read it from where she stood, but daren't speak. She whispered, 'Hold on.'

'Speak up. I can't hear you.'

He'd hear her scream, when Ferretface shot her, she thought. She made a great play of listening, back-view. If they looked, her black skirt and stupid shoes were bound to give her away. She turned her head away from them, just as Mrs Turkin came out of the Ladies. Their eyes met. Perhaps, Nutty thought, fear had transformed her features, for Mrs Turkin looked right through her. She joined the men and they moved towards the car park.

'Are you still there?' Nutty hissed.

There was a clicking noise and a long silence. He had gone for his coffee, no doubt. Nutty screamed into the mouthpiece, 'Come back! I want to tell you—'

She saw the three Russians reach the car. The man got out the car key and Nutty saw Mrs Turkin's face suddenly go berserk: she shouted something and turned round, pointing in Nutty's direction. Tired as she was, the penny had obviously dropped.

Russian expletives! Ferretface turned, and Nutty saw his murderer's eyes meet hers. He started to run. Nutty screamed into the telephone, dropped it and ran.

She leapt through the swing doors and flung them back violently behind her, right into Ferret-face as he came. She ran through the café, past the amazed queue at the counter and out through an open window at the end, taking it like a hurdler.

'Oh, Christian, Christian, save me!'

But now she was on the far side of the camp away from the car park, in among the tents fixed to the sides of cars, some with whole kitchens attached, and chairs and tables. People cooking their lunches stared in amazement. She dodged in and out, found an empty tent and plunged in. She could hear screams coming from the restaurant, and a crash of chairs. Could the Russians hurdle through the window as nippily as she? She doubted it. She yanked at the bottom of her tent on the far side, pulling out the peg, and wriggled out on the far side, leaving the soggy anorak behind. In and out of the tents, she kept her head down and ran, making round for the front of the restaurant again. There were screams all round now – the Russians must be disturbing a few of the lunch-cookers, crouched over their barbecues.

'Christian, where are you?'

She had kept to her circle and was now running

down the side of the restaurant towards the car park. Christian was sitting there on his horse, holding hers, like a true cowboy to the rescue.

'Here!'

She leapt forward and grabbed her horse's mane. Christian leaned over its back from the far side and held out his hand. She would never have got on without his desperate heave, but she was up and her heels drumming into the horse's sides. Up the road they galloped, faster than they had ever come down, the horses sensing the urgency, until they were over the brow at the top.

They pulled back to a slow canter.

'They'll go now. We've blown it! The police'll never get up here in time.'

'You got a message through?'

'Yes. Half a message at least. Where we are, and what they did. He said, was I one of the joy-riders—'

'You are now,' Christian said. He laughed. 'Nutty – nutter – you've got the right name.'

'They'll get away now! They know I was talking to the police—'

'They won't,' Christian said.

'Why not?'

'There was a bloke coming up the track, a back-packer, and I asked him if he had a knife and he produced one and I stuck it through their tyres. He was a bit surprised but I told him it was in a good cause. I told him it was a murderer's getaway car. He didn't believe me, of course.'

'No-one'll believe us! I wouldn't believe it myself, if anyone told me.'

'Tony saw. We've got witnesses.'

'They never give up. I hope the police are on their way.'

They rode slowly back along the track, until they would meet the rest of the party. At last, it seemed peaceful and beautiful and all as it should be, with the sun shining and the strong wind dropping to a lovely fresh zephyr and the bees buzzing in the heather buds. Christian and Nutty relaxed, enjoying the feel of the horses' warm movement beneath them and the feel of the sun in their faces.

CHAPTER ELEVEN

Arnold, John Pike and Christian were taken to hospital; Jodie, Nutty and Hoomey to the police station. Tony went with them. Mrs Knox and Mr Harlech arrived in a great fluster, with Boris in the back of their car, and Mr and Mrs Turkin and Ferretface were rounded up and taken to the same police station.

Hoomey dozed off during the questioning and fell off his chair, but the two girls told their tale with admirable clarity. Mrs Knox sat listening, opening and shutting her mouth with consternation.

'I knew it, I knew it! That boy! I know I saw a boy who shouldn't be there—'

'Arnold has been incredibly brave,' Jodie said doggedly. 'If it wasn't for him, nobody would know—'

'It all has to be proved, young lady,' the police officer warned. 'We can't prefer charges until—'

'You can about their trying to kill us!'

'All in good time. We have to get the facts.'

'It's true that Boris had a different manager when we met him in Russia and, I understand, when he was met off the plane at Heathrow,' Mrs Knox said. 'If only he could speak some English! Is there nobody – a Russian speaker—?'

'We are looking for one now. There's a teacher at a school in Inverness – we are trying to contact him.'

'And there's a body in the lake at home. You must find that,' Jodie put in.

If it hadn't been for Tony's evidence, in clipped army style, the two girls doubted if their story would have been believed. Even then, there was a suggestion that they had been joy-riding and gone out of control. Hoomey, kicked hard on the ankle by Nutty, gave his tale of going to the Gents with Arnold and seeing Ferretface abduct him, forcing him into the Citroen.

'We took Miss Manners' car to chase him – it's still up there by the bothy, by Antrim Falls. That's evidence!'

'Just keep to your statement,' the policeman said doggedly. 'We've got as far as your getting a lift with Miss Manners to the concert. Now . . .'

It took hours. Even Nutty was getting confused by the end of the afternoon when they were allowed to go home. The Turkins and

Ferretface were being held overnight, and the Russian teacher was to arrive to talk to Boris the following day. Tony ·had gone back to his trail-riders, to get back on course. Boris was to come home in the car with Mrs Knox and the three of them and return to the police station the following morning. The others were to stay in hospital overnight and be let out in the morning if declared fit.

'Thank goodness we've no concert tonight!' Mrs Knox exclaimed as she set off on the drive back. 'No solo clarinet, no timpanist, the string leader—' she glanced in her driving mirror and saw Jodie dozing in the back seat '—suffering from exhaustion . . . the soloist from nerves . . . '

Boris clearly had no idea what was going on. He hadn't been allowed to speak to his minders, but had realized that they were being held by the police.

'The KGB,' Nutty tried to tell him.

She kept falling asleep in mid-sentence.

The following morning Mrs Knox drove Boris back again to meet the Russian teacher. She collected the three boys, discharged from hospital, and took them to the police station to make their statements. Arnold was the star witness. Having such a good story for once, he told no lies, and late in the afternoon news came through from East Anglia that a body had been found in the lake, weighted down with a sledge-hammer and a five-gallon drum of diesel fuel. Arnold was vindicated.

Boris was deeply shocked. Even without the Russian teacher to tell them, they could all see his distressed state. Distressed about his dead minder, they gathered, not his current bunch. The Russian teacher told them that he wanted to stay in England. He said he hated the Turkins. He wanted to stay with his new friends and play piano with the schools orchestra. For ever.

'We're none of us for ever,' Christian said regretfully.

But Boris came back to their tranquil dormitory and in the evening they all lazed on their beds, washed up after their adventures. Arnold felt miraculously freed of his burdens, with Mrs Knox's blessings upon him, bed and food guaranteed for the rest of the holiday. He was on a high, and kept thinking of clashing cymbals. How come he could get a job like Nutty's? A newspaper reporter wanted to speak to him. He went downstairs in a daze.

'What's going to happen to Arnie?' Nutty said sadly. 'When we get back? Surely he hasn't got to go back to that school—'

They locked the doors, Arnold said. Even the Gasworks, workaday, paint-peeling school that it was, was cheerful and perfectly bearable.

'He can come and live with me,' Jodie said, 'and Boris. We've got six bedrooms and a housekeeper and a cook and my dad's hardly ever at home. He'll be pleased. He likes me to have friends in.'

The others were impressed, Nutty and Hoomey openly.

'How come he doesn't mind?' Nutty tried to think of her father having Boris and Arnold to live with them, just like that, and couldn't really see it. She and her sister Gloria had to share a bedroom as it was.

'My dad's got a guilt conscience,' Jodie said. 'Being away all the time, playing tennis, and my ma sort of – well, gone off.' She blushed. Jodie seemed transparently none the worse for her deprivations. 'I'd like a pianist around – it'd be great, playing together.'

'You could teach him English.'

'Make a trio, with Arnie on cymbals,' Nutty said.

'Arnie's great,' John Pike said. 'You should've heard him, Nutty, right on the bong every time, and never done it before. He got quite carried away.'

'Tons better than you, Nutty,' Hoomey said endearingly.

'Well, I only stood in for my friend, then she got chickenpox with complications and never came back and there I was, lumbered. I only did it to

183

oblige, not because I wanted to. If Arnie wants my job he's welcome. After this holiday, mind. I'm not going home while he stays!'

'You'd have to clear it with Mr Harlech,' John Pike said. 'But he won't mind tuppence if Arnie's good. Which he is.'

'He could have a go in the rehearsal tomorrow. See how he does.'

The next day Arnold had his picture in the newspaper and the story was on the front page. He hoped Aunt Margaret would read it and know he was safe (safe?). She was bound to have heard about the body in the lake and would no doubt be thinking, 'If only I had believed him!' . . . If he had had any money he might have rung her up . . . but as it was he was far more excited by the news that Mr Harlech had agreed that he could take Nutty's place on the cymbals. Nutty took him in hand, to teach him.

'There's more to it than just crashing them together,' she said tartly. 'Any fool can do that. If you're going to do it properly . . . '

She took him off to one of the practice rooms and Hoomey trailed along to ting accompaniment on his triangle. Christian wanted to practise but was worried about Boris, lying on the bed looking sadly at the ceiling.

Jodie said, 'It's dreadful for him: he can't even talk about it.'

'What can we do?'

Jodie went to her room and fetched her violin and some sheets of music and showed them to Boris. She pointed sternly.

'You – and me—'

He sat up and smiled. Jodie led him out to the practice room with the best piano in it where the boy using it graciously gave way to his superiors. Boris sat down and Jodie put the music in front of him. She knew it was a colossal cheek to think she could play violin well enough to invite Boris to accompany her but she also knew perfectly well that a good music work-out could soothe – or at least distract – the troubled mind. It was difficult to think music again, after all the excitements of the preceding two days. It seemed like two years!

She picked up her violin. Boris straightened the music on the rack and sat with his hands at the ready, poised over the keyboard like a pair of gigantic white spiders. He turned towards her and gave her an eager, enchanting smile. I could get on with this guy, Jodie thought, with a sudden swing of excitement. She felt her adrenalin flowing, her hands trembling with a desire to produce notes as fluently as Boris, to lift her talent on to another plane ... she had a chance, and a future, if Boris wanted a friend. She laughed, and gave Boris the nod to start.

But Arnold, although grateful for the invitation, couldn't see himself as a living-in cymbalist in the boringest place in the world, East Anglia.

'What 'm I going to do?' he asked Nutty, now that the adventure was over.

'Mrs Knox said you could stay, right till the end.'

'But then?'

Nutty was old enough and experienced enough to know that life ground on, good and bad and inbetween, and there was no getting away from it.

'You've got friends now,' she said. 'You didn't seem to have any before.'

'No.'

'Bonus one. You've discovered you've got a talent.'

'Have I?'

'Yes. A natural sense of rhythm, timing – that's a large chunk towards being a musician. When I explained the music to you – those blobs between the bar-lines – you picked it up no trouble. Two four time, three four, six eight – some people find that hard. Bonus two.'

'Hmm.'

'If you play your cards right, influential adults feel grateful towards you – for uncovering the crime about Boris. Bonus three. They might want to help you.'

'How can they?'

'They can tell the police how useful you've been. The police will be nice to you – you've done all that work for them. Think about it. That body in the lake was bound to have been discovered sooner or later, and they'd have had no idea who it was or why. Just think – you've handed it to them on a plate. The police are bound to like you now. Bonus four.'

'They might let me off the other things? Like a grass gets let off?'

'Yes. You can count on it.'

'Hmm.'

Arnold did not dispute that the four bonuses were pretty good, but in the end it made no difference to the fact that he had to go back to London and get on with his unsatisfactory life.

Nutty said, quite vehemently, 'But it's no different for you than anyone else, is it? It's what you make of it. Hoomey's got everything, and has made nothing. You've got nothing, but you're not doing too pretty damned badly at the moment. Mrs Knox lives in London – she'll get you into a youth orchestra if you want it badly enough. You've just got to decide to go for it, keep your nose clean. You're clever, you're sharp – you can make it if you want to.'

She was the first one who'd ever told him so. His spirits lifted considerably. Nutty had a sort of strength that transmitted. What did she have after all, for a girl, with her strong, square shape and her corkscrew hair sticking out as if she'd had an electric shock? No boy in his right mind would want to take her out to show off to his mates. But Arnold's instincts told him that Nutty got by, and very well too, on far more enduring qualities than mere prettiness, and if he had her for a friend he wouldn't go far wrong.

'I've got you too,' he said.

'Bonus five,' said Nutty.

THE END